"GET BEHIND THE TREE," BRAND ORDERED.

Without warning, he pulled her toward the nearest tree and pushed her easily against it, covering her body with his own.

His fingers were wrapped around the soft, sensitive flesh of her shoulders, and his chest moved rhythmically against hers with every breath he took. His thigh was locked provocatively between her legs, making it impossible to move.

His skin was surprisingly soft against her, and gave off a musky, male scent that was sultry, disconcerting, and undeniably erotic. Undeniably male.

Faline took a deep breath, but it only made matters worse. She couldn't shake off the scent of *him.* And she couldn't deny the effect he was having on her. "Get your paws off me, *now*, Weston, or I make my self-defense teacher proud."

His eyes flickered with interest as he looked down at her, faintly mocking. "What's the matter, Wildcat? Afraid?"

Her green eyes flashed. "Hell, no, I'm not afraid."

He tilted her chin up toward him and she wondered what he would do next. "You should be afraid," he said softly. "Some forces in nature are so primitive, they can never be controlled. There's no defense against them. . . ."

WHAT ARE *LOVESWEPT* ROMANCES?

They are stories of true romance and touching emotion. We believe those two very important ingredients are constants in our highly sensual and very believable stories in the LOVESWEPT *line. Our goal is to give you, the reader, stories of consistently high quality that may sometimes make you laugh, sometimes make you cry, but are always fresh and creative and contain many delightful surprises within their pages.*

Most romance fans read an enormous number of books. Those they truly love, they keep. Others may be traded with friends and soon forgotten. We hope that each LOVESWEPT *romance will be a treasure—a "keeper." We will always try to publish*

LOVE STORIES YOU'LL NEVER FORGET
BY AUTHORS YOU'LL ALWAYS REMEMBER

The Editors

Loveswept® 785

UNTAMED

CYNTHIA POWELL

BANTAM BOOKS
NEW YORK · TORONTO · LONDON · SYDNEY · AUCKLAND

UNTAMED

A Bantam Book / April 1996

ISBN 0-553-44548-0

Published simultaneously in the United States and Canada

Bantam Books are published by Bantam Books, a division of Bantam Doubleday Dell Publishing Group, Inc. Its trademark, consisting of the words "Bantam Books" and the portrayal of a rooster, is Registered in U.S. Patent and Trademark Office and in other countries. Marca Registrada. Bantam Books, 1540 Broadway, New York, New York 10036.

PRINTED IN THE UNITED STATES OF AMERICA

OPM 0 9 8 7 6 5 4 3 2 1

PROLOGUE

When Brand Weston saw the tiger running toward him at full speed, he threw back his head and laughed. The ferocious, four-hundred-pound beast knocked him to the ground, and together they tumbled, head over paw in the warm Florida sunshine. This was Brand's favorite way to spend an afternoon.

The tiger seemed to enjoy it, too, and although there was ample opportunity to eat the man alive, something about Brand made the big cat refrain from biting his head off. Fang, as the tiger was tenderly called, knew better than to provoke his master.

Although the tiger was terrifying to look at, the man could be equally intimidating. His body, bronzed and bare to the waist, had the bold, primitive beauty of raw masculine power. His lion's mane of long hair was caught in the back with a leather cord, pulled away from a strong, unshaven face and a pair of searing amber eyes.

In another era, the man might've killed the tiger, and worn the striped skin as a symbol of power. But this man preferred to befriend it, and to live beside the tiger in peace. Brand knew there was greater power in that.

As evening approached, he heard the lions growling in the sultry summer air, circling, snarling in frustration. One of the females was in heat, and the two males, restless and aroused, were vying for dominance. Brand swore softly, trying to distract himself, but the strange, guttural sounds persisted. Nothing could block the eerie noise of the two big cats, ready to consummate. And nothing could remind him so readily that it'd been far too long since he'd taken a mate himself.

This momentary desire he felt would probably pass before long. If not, there were women willing enough to appease it. Women who didn't want to mate for life.

Human females seldom came to Wildacre Ranch and when they did, they stayed for only a short time. Despite his temporary discomfort, Brand was determined to keep it that way. This place was too tough for most women to take, too removed from town entertainment, and especially on nights like this one, far too dangerous.

Untamed

3

"Lions and tigers? Man-eating cats? Faline, are you out of your obstinate mind?"

Faline Eastbrook carefully stowed her telephoto lens in its padded case, placing it gingerly in her large camera bag along with the rest of her portable equipment. She sat back and stared at her silver-haired agent across the cool, barren expanse of her New York photography studio.

Vail D'Argent was pacing the polished wood floors, too fastidious to sit down for fear that it might wrinkle his perfectly pressed silk suit.

"I don't want to *tame* the tigers, Vail," Faline said calmly. "Just to photograph them. *Eco* magazine needs shots for a series they've written on exotic animals. They've arranged some sort of deal with this Brand Weston fellow to photograph the big cats he keeps on his Florida ranch."

Vail stopped pacing and gave her his most disapproving stare. "*Wildman* Weston? That recluse who lives with lions? Faline, sweetie, you're killing me. How *could* you accept an assignment like that?"

Faline brushed the fall of smooth brown hair from her face and smiled at the expected theatrics. "Call it a crazy quirk I have, but when an editor offers me a job, I'm happy to take it. Even with a smaller publication like *Eco*." She pointed to the half-empty filing cabinet in the corner that she'd bought her first week in business to organize the customer accounts. "In case you haven't noticed, the work has been getting a bit scarce around here lately. When Scott skipped out on us, he took most of the plum assignments with him."

Vail cringed, shuddering at the mere mention of the name. "Just stab me in the heart why don't you, Faline? If I hadn't set you two up as partners, this never would've happened." He slumped into a chair and hung his head in abject anguish, the silk suit temporarily forgotten. "I'll never get over it."

Faline swallowed hard, fighting back a wave of bitterness. She doubted either of them would ever get over what Scott McKenzie had done. First, he'd pretended to be Faline's friend. Later, he'd played the part of a faithful lover. Too late, she'd realized that he was neither. He'd left the studio a month ago, taking most of the steady clients with him.

He'd done his best to ruin the hardworking reputation she'd built over the last eight years in the business. But he hadn't entirely succeeded. Not while there was a single person left still willing to hire her. Not while she had the grit to keep going.

Resolutely, she damped the anger back down and quickly closed the zipper on her camera bag. "Forget it, Vail. It's time to put that episode behind us and move on. This Florida job will be a new challenge, a new beginning. The pay's pretty low, but at this point I'm lucky to be working at all. I don't have much wildlife experience. *Eco* took a chance on me because they need the job done yesterday and most of the bigger names already turned them down. And I *need* to work, Vail. Besides, getting out of New York for a while will probably do me a lot of good."

Vail twisted his neatly manicured hands in frustration. "But you *can't* leave New York to go chasing after a bunch of wild beasts. You're a city girl. One hundred percent urbanite. You'd never survive. Besides, stalking lions and tigers with a camera isn't an assignment, darling, it's suicide."

Faline folded her arms across her chest, and gave her agent a long, hard look. Maybe he was right. The episode with Scott had warped her judgment about business—about a lot of things. Maybe all that hurt really had made her crazy.

Along with Scott's betrayal, she'd lost a lot of her so-called friends. The crowd she'd met at art school had stood by her at the beginning of her career. They'd been there to share her small successes—the time she'd landed her first paying assignment, the moment the word *photographer* had been neatly painted on the gallery door, just below her name. They'd all been there to help her celebrate.

But she'd been younger then, and a lot more naive. Now, at twenty-eight, with her professional popularity at an all-time low, there was no one around to help her grieve. Now, when she needed support the most, she was on her own. That same crowd had shaken their heads over her breakup with Scott, then moved on to celebrate with someone else. Someone who was on their way up, instead of down.

Her father and mother, both lifelong employees in the same stable insurance firm, had patted her on the cheek and suggested it was time for her to find a "real job." Only Vail had stuck with her through it all, urging her to keep working. But due to her current lack of trust in people, she cynically connected his loyalty to a tidy ten percent commission.

"Trust me, kiddo," Vail added softly, flicking a speck of dust from his sharply pointed lapel. "I'll find you something better soon."

Trust me. If only he hadn't said that, he might've convinced her to stay, but Faline doubted she'd ever learn to trust again. *Trust me.* Funny, Scott had often said the same thing. This time, she decided, the mistakes or rewards would be hers alone. She would learn to live by her own instincts and not by those of any man.

"I'm not backing down on this one, Vail. I expect you to contact the people at *Eco* to make the necessary arrangements."

Vail leaned back in his chair and refused to make eye contact, staring at the ceiling in hurt resignation. "Go then," he told her bluntly. "I'll negotiate terms with the magazine, but don't expect me to come save you when the lions decide to eat you alive."

But Faline wasn't afraid. The beasts in New York had already had their fill of her. What harm could a few wild animals in Florida do?

ONE

"There it is, lady, Wildacre Ranch—better known as the Lion's Den. I hope you've got a whip and a chair in one of those bags you brought."

Faline leaned forward in her seat, trying to make out the view beyond the dusty cab windshield. According to the driver, she had just arrived. In the middle of nowhere.

Twenty miles from anything resembling a town, the property paralleled a sand and gravel road, cutting through a shaded forest of white pine, oak, and palmettos. A tall wire fence surrounded the land, and spring-blooming azalea bushes jutted here and there, soft and showy in their early evening shades of pink, mauve, and magenta. At least the ranch didn't *look* dangerous.

"Would you mind pulling up to the house, please?"

The cabbie skeptically surveyed the formidable

fence and tall iron gate through which his vehicle would have to pass. "No way," he said, after a moment's indecision. "I've got a wife and kids at home."

Faline counted out the fare, handed it to the driver, and let herself and her luggage out of the taxi. The car did a three-point turn at the base of the long driveway, but the driver stopped momentarily, apparently trying to clear his conscience. "I hope you understand, lady. People don't go in that place. At least, no one ever sees 'em come *out* again. Sure you want me to leave you here?"

No, Faline answered to herself, *I'm not.* She wondered what the man would do if she threw herself in front of the cab and begged him to take her back to the airport. Based on his opinion of the place, he'd probably be sympathetic, but bolting back to New York at this point wasn't only cowardly, it simply wasn't an option.

"I'll be fine," she assured the driver, then felt a sudden jolt of regret as he shook his head and obligingly drove off down the deserted stretch of road. So that was it. She'd finish the job, or die trying. Hopefully such extreme measures wouldn't be necessary.

The heavy gate posed something of a problem, but Faline managed to unlatch it and let herself inside the forested front yard. It was still a long walk up to the house, and she steeled herself for the spooky trek through the shadowy woods. She opted to leave her luggage on the spot but clung instinctively to her purse and small camera bag. Taking a few steps forward, she stopped again, startled by a faint rustling noise in a stand of bushes beyond.

She glanced quickly around, but couldn't quite place the sound. Hesitating, she walked on, her pulse increasing with her pace.

"Don't move."

The low voice came out of nowhere and nearly startled Faline out of her stockings. She couldn't have moved if she'd wanted to, but her self-defense training soon kicked into gear, and she knew exactly what to do next. Scream.

Faline's reaction was quick, but the man behind her was quicker. He pulled her against him, locking her arms from behind, and clamped a hand down over her mouth before she could make a sound.

"Hush," he whispered in a low growl. "I'm not going to hurt you, but you've got to stay quiet. Stop squirming, you little hellcat. I'm going to take my hand off your mouth, but if you make one sound, we're both going to regret it. Understand?"

Faline quit struggling for a second, and nodded her compliance. She had every intention of screaming once the maniac's hand was removed, and a few other ideas about which body parts to kick, but she never got the chance. As she whirled around to face him, her legs grew weak and the sound died in her throat.

She could do little more than stare at the man

in front of her, a man who did not have the face of a maniac. He had the hard, unrefined beauty of a sculpture cast in bronze, the rough, sensuous lines of some ancient work of art that had been hidden from human eyes for centuries. For an instant, Faline felt as though she'd made a miraculous discovery. Then the sculpture spoke.

"Faline Eastbrook?"

It took her a few moments to nod and another few to realize who this man must be. Wildman Weston. Not exactly the gray-bearded, wild-eyed hermit she'd expected. This guy was in his early thirties, with a sleek mane of sun-lightened hair and an intense gaze that held the watchful look of a tribal warrior.

His golden eyes gleamed back at her, curious, searching. It was a primal, uncivilized stare that no man in New York would have dared to give her. Faline couldn't help bristling. It was a look that held more warning than welcome.

"Brand Weston," he said bluntly, holding out his hand. "You're on Wildacre Ranch."

Faline automatically shook his hand, but the gesture seemed oddly out of place, a trivial, almost ridiculous formality after the physical contact they'd already shared.

"You have a strange way of greeting your guests, Mr. Weston. I'm not used to being grabbed from behind. Is that some sort of local Southern custom I'm not aware of?"

His smile was an even bigger shock. It was like

seeing the first shafts of sunlight streak across the morning sky. Faline's breath caught in her throat, and she realized that although this man had turned out not to be an attacker, he still might be very dangerous.

"And you have a strange way of not following instructions, Ms. Eastbrook. You were told to drive directly to the house."

She bridled at the challenge in his tone. The rugged roughneck might have the advantage of an awesome face, but he was way behind in the hospitality department. Clearly, he didn't intend to put her at ease or offer polite apologies. Still, there was something straightforward in his manner, something bold and unpretentious that she had to admire.

He'd spoken plainly enough. Faline felt free to do the same. She was a professional, after all, with some experience at dealing with difficult people. To win the respect of a man like that, you had to stick up for yourself.

"I don't see what that has to do with . . ."

But her comments fell on deaf ears. Weston wasn't paying the slightest bit of attention to her anymore. Instead, his gaze was riveted to the thick patch of bushes behind her, to the very spot where she'd heard the strange sound. She turned briefly to see if anything was there, but no sign of life appeared. Nothing but a few green leaves, shimmering in the fading light.

She turned back to face him again. "Mr. Weston?"

He held her at arm's length, cautioning her to stand still, then put two fingers over his mouth, demanding her silence.

Faline began to wonder if the guy's brain was in complete working order. Certainly, the rest of him seemed to be okay. In fact, the man appeared to be in peak physical condition.

He towered over her by nearly six inches, putting her almost at eye level with his chest. A chest that was undeniably well developed, suntanned, and shamelessly bare. The sinewed muscles snaked down a flat stomach and disappeared into the waistband of his well-worn blue jeans. Except for a few tears at the knees and some suspicious shred marks over the left thigh, those jeans were the only clue that linked the man to modern civilization.

Savage, untamed, predatory. Those were the words that came to mind. Definitely not crazy. She should be able to reason with him, in a calm, conscientious manner.

"Now then, Mr. Weston . . ."

"Get behind the tree."

Without warning, he pulled her toward the nearest tree and pushed her easily against it, covering her body with his own.

Faline's heart began to pound wildly. What was going on here? This man she'd just met, a stranger really, was treating her in a most shocking way. And for all her training in sticky business situations and photography field tactics, she wasn't sure how to stop him.

He wrapped his fingers around the soft, sensitive flesh of her shoulders, and his chest moved rhythmically against hers with every breath he took. His thigh was locked provocatively between her legs, making it impossible to move. She was trapped. By some Tarzan without a T-shirt. And she didn't like it one bit.

"Get your paws off me, *now*, Weston, or I'll make my self-defense teacher proud."

His eyes flickered with interest as he looked down at her, his words faintly mocking. "What's wrong, Wildcat? Afraid?"

Faline's green eyes flashed at the suggestion. "Hell no, I'm not afraid." She stopped momentarily to catch her breath and noticed his gaze had strayed back to the thick stand of bushes. "Afraid of what?"

He tilted her chin toward him, and Faline let herself be guided by his touch, wondering what he would do next.

"You should be afraid." His voice was a quiet murmur against her cheek. "This ranch is no place for a lady. You never know what's waiting for you, maybe just around the next tree."

He let go of her chin and turned his mouth to whisper in her ear. "Hold very still, Ms. Eastbrook. Fang doesn't like having strangers at the ranch."

Fang? She felt a cold chill creep down her spine

and knew that this time it wasn't from Weston's touch. She turned her head again to the dense foliage and saw what his overdeveloped caveman senses had detected all along. A pair of large gleaming eyes stared back at her, glowing in the gathering darkness. Tiger eyes.

Instinctively, she moved closer to Brand, and asked faintly, "He's loose?"

He didn't need to answer. Clearly, the tiger was free, but Brand seemed more interested in her reaction to the animal. Faline looked up at him, shivering in spite of the heat, and all at once she understood. Wildman Weston wasn't crazy at all. In fact, he seemed to be enjoying himself. Not from the pleasure of holding her in his arms, but from the expression of fear he read on her face. He *wanted* her to be afraid.

For some reason, he was trying to scare her. He'd gone to great lengths to protect her, sheltering her body with his. He didn't intend to let the tiger harm her, but all the same, he wanted her to be aware of the danger.

Faline willed herself to stop trembling. No matter how terrified she felt, she was determined not to let it show. Weston would soon learn that she didn't frighten so easily.

She raised her chin a notch, smiling sweetly at him. "In New York," she said coolly, "we eat tigers like that for breakfast."

Brand couldn't help grinning a bit at that one. He hadn't expected the slick city chick to be so gutsy. He kind of liked that defiant look in her eye, even though he knew she was quaking underneath. Fang usually had that effect on people, but Ms. Eastbrook had the bravado not to show it.

Curious now, and intrigued by her spirit, he tested her reaction again. "He's probably thinking the same thing about you. Shall I let go now?"

She eyed the tiger warily, then loosened her hold on Brand. "He'd find me a poor meal, I'm sure. Too tough."

Another smile softened Brand's features. The lady had called his bluff. She'd decided to brazen it out, which meant she was either reckless, or adventurous to the core. Both were dangerous.

Even more disturbing was the look of sheer determination in her eyes. She had a clear purpose in coming here—to photograph his animals. For the sake of his cats, and for the promotion of their cause, he'd chosen to allow it. But having a woman like her around the ranch was more than he'd bargained for.

He'd relaxed his rule for this one. Strangers normally weren't allowed at Wildacre and even though Ms. Eastbrook might have a job to do, she'd have to do it quick. She might be an interesting distraction, but to a man who preferred to live alone, distractions weren't always welcome.

Or maybe it was the look of vulnerability about her that bothered him. He could read it in her eyes, hear it in her voice, sense it in the careful, cautious way she held herself. The lady was all bottled up inside, all protective and pulled back, the way his animals usually were when they first arrived.

And that was the part of her he found the most intriguing. The part she didn't want to share. The part he would never allow himself to explore, because he didn't intend to let her hang around too long.

Fang made another movement in the bushes, and Faline's heart leapt to her throat. Instinctively, she closed both eyes and waited for the worst, but when it didn't come, she opened them again to see Weston grinning at her. She narrowed her gaze at him, failing to see the humor in the situation. There was hardly anything funny about a free-roaming tiger with food fantasies.

"Can't you put him on a leash or something?" she asked, glaring.

"Sure thing, Wildcat," he said. "Did you want to take him for a walk?"

Faline chose to ignore the sarcasm. "I was thinking you might walk him yourself. Away from here."

"Poor Fang," Brand replied, talking to the tiger. "I don't think the lady wants you around."

In response to his master's voice, Fang raised himself up on all fours, his tail swishing back and forth with fierce feline anticipation.

"You see," Brand said, watching the wide-eyed expression on Faline's face. "He likes you."

Sure, Faline thought, *as an appetizer.* "Nice

kitty," she answered out loud, acutely conscious that Fang was a far cry from a house cat. One was big enough to eat you. The other wasn't.

"It's time for his feeding," Brand told her, as if that explained the eager look in the big cat's eye. "Meet me up at the house," he said curtly, "but don't expect the red-carpet treatment. It's not some swanky hotel."

An unfair remark, Faline decided, since she'd expected no such thing. In fact, swanky wasn't at all her style. Her very average-sized apartment was far from luxurious. So why was Weston provoking her so deliberately?

Before she had a chance to figure it out, her tormentor spoke a few quick words to the big cat, and led him off through the woods. Faline watched them go with mixed relief and amazement. Weston's hand was at the beast's big collar, guiding him along, and except for the animal's size, and the lack of a trusty leash or plastic pooper-scooper, it looked as easy as walking a dog.

Until Fang let out a deep growl. No pooch she'd ever met could make a noise like that. Faline shuddered, and as quietly as she could, retrieved her purse and camera bag and hurried to the house.

TWO

To Faline's surprise, Brand's home wasn't a hut suspended in the trees, but a large plantation-style two-story, with warm lights beckoning her to enter. The front door was unlocked, and she didn't wait for a formal invitation. Never had she felt so eager to be indoors.

She tossed her bags on a hall bench and sank down beside them, more shaken than she cared to admit. But before she'd had a chance to look around, or acclimate to the new surroundings, the front door opened, and Brand walked in. So much for her moment of peace. It was impossible to relax with a man like him nearby.

He'd brought the rest of her luggage and dropped it at the bottom of the polished wood staircase. "Planning a prolonged stay, Ms. Eastbrook? It looks like you packed enough clothes for a month."

Faline leaned back against the bench and crossed her arms, ready for battle. It was becoming all too clear that Weston wanted to get rid of her quick. Well, the feeling was mutual. She didn't intend to stay a minute longer than was absolutely necessary, but she wouldn't let him push her out before the job was finished.

She needed this job. For her personal satisfaction as well as her professional survival. It was time to prove that she could make it on her own, without Scott, without anyone. If Weston believed he could bully her into leaving prematurely, he'd seriously underestimated his new houseguest.

"Two weeks," she answered curtly, resting her hands calmly in her lap. "I can complete the shoot by then as long as I have your cooperation."

"Cooperation?" He folded his corded arms across the wide expanse of his chest and leaned back against the stair rail, watching her. "Exactly what kind of cooperation did you have in mind, woman? Want me to hold your hand and promise that the nice kitties won't bite it off? Or maybe you were expecting the deluxe tour—the one with the air-conditioned Jeep and the tape-recorded nature spiel so you can have a nice, safe, synthetic experience?"

"Don't get your biceps in a bind," she shot back smoothly. "And *don't* call me woman. I *am* one, of course, but not the kind you seem to think. I won't need any hand-holding."

Definitely not from him anyway, she added silently. Grabbing that tiger by the paw would be far more preferable. And a lot less dangerous.

"Although the nature spiel would be nice," she allowed, reconsidering. "I'll bet you really know your stuff. According to *Eco*, you're an expert in the big feline field. Biology training at the graduate level, right?"

He narrowed his eyes at her. "Sounds like you've done your homework."

"I asked a few questions," she admitted. "I wanted to make sure you knew what you were doing. In case you haven't noticed, there's some risk involved in this assignment. You can't expect me to put my safety on the line without knowing anything about you."

He studied her another moment, as though he were considering the truth of her statement. Faline met his gaze openly, matching him stare for stare. She couldn't help feeling it was a test of some sort. As if he could read her inside based on what the outside of her was doing.

He finally released his visual hold on her, apparently satisfied with her reaction. Or simply tired of the game. Faline wasn't sure which.

"I have a graduate degree," he told her, "if that's what you want to know. But academics aren't going to protect you here. This is the place where gut instinct comes into play. As much as humans might want them to, animals don't always act by the book. They're *wild* animals after all. That's what makes them interesting."

Untamed

21

Faline swallowed hard, realizing some humans could be fascinating in much the same way. The man in front of her, for instance. She doubted he did anything by the book.

"Anyway," he added, keeping his voice low and even, "graduate school was some time ago. I haven't been back to the university in over a dozen years."

Faline wondered if that was when he'd holed himself up with his animals and left society behind. Twelve years—it was a long time to be alone. Or maybe he hadn't been. Maybe he had a Jane stashed around the ranch somewhere. Some very brave, incredibly strong, intrepid woman she just hadn't met yet.

"So you live here by yourself?" she asked, somewhat hesitant to pry. Weston wasn't exactly the chatty type. She didn't know how he'd take to the current line of conversation.

He nodded briefly. "More or less."

"Isn't it a little hard to run this place alone? I mean, without a partner. Or a wife?"

He lifted his eyebrows at her. "You're starting to sound more like a reporter than a photographer, Ms. Eastbrook. Or, if we're going to get personal here, maybe I should call you Faline."

"Sorry. Just curious."

He shrugged. "I get along. I have a woman who comes in to take care of the place. The animals are my responsibility."

I have a woman. Not a very romantic way to put

it, Faline decided. Probably an employee, she surmised, based on Brand's brief description of the lady. So there wasn't a Jane around after all.

Night was settling in around them now, and eerie, unfamiliar noises sounded in the dark beyond the door. Frogs and insects and a bird of some sort, crying in the forest outside. It was a peaceful chorus, a cacophony of tropical woodland creatures, but a little strange and sad.

Faline hugged her arms to her chest, comforting herself against the feeling. It was probably a normal reaction, after leaving a city filled with so many people for an entirely new environment where there were only two. She wondered if Brand noticed it, too, the atmosphere of sheer solitude and isolation. She looked over at him, and their eyes locked and held.

"Don't you ever get lonely?" she asked him softly.

At first glance, it was hard to imagine that he did. He was large and strong—the most blatantly *masculine* man she'd ever met. Sturdy, stubborn, and self-sufficient. Clearly the kind of guy who could take care of himself.

But it didn't make sense why a man so obviously in the prime of life would choose to live in such secluded privacy. Didn't every human being crave company at some time or another? What would make a person *want* to live all alone?

He took a long time to answer. So long, in fact, that Faline began to wonder if she'd overstepped her bounds once again. When he finally spoke, it was short and straight to the point.

"I've adjusted to the remoteness. Most people don't."

"Most people?" she asked. Was he referring to her, challenging her staying power? Or possibly referring to someone else?

"Most *women*," he added. "So I hope you're tougher than you look. I never had a wife, but I did have a fiancée once—" He hesitated, reluctant to continue. "She barely lasted two months," he finally finished.

A fiancée? Faline tried to imagine her, wondering what kind of woman Weston would choose. It sounded like he'd picked one who wasn't too fond of rural life. Or maybe he was simply trying to scare her off again, to make her leave him alone and in peace. Peace from what, she wasn't sure. She was only sure that she *had* to stay. For now.

"Two months," she repeated. "Then surely I should be able to make it for two weeks."

"Maybe," he admitted. "But Katrina was here *before* I took in any of the big cats."

Faline wasn't sure how to answer that one. He was testing her again, baiting her just to see how easily she would frighten. She felt the frustration welling up inside her. Why was he making it so hard?

Brand watched the emotions flooding across her face and swore softly under his breath. He hadn't meant to push her so hard. God, he didn't think he could take it if she went all warm and weepy on him now. He was sorry if he'd hurt her. Real sorry. The last thing he needed on his hands at the moment was another creature in need of comfort.

"Never mind," he told her gruffly. "I just want you to know what you're up against. It's not an easy place to live."

He wanted to add that he wasn't an easy person to live with, but didn't bother. She was here on a temporary basis, no more. He didn't have to tell her that he'd been bad news for females his entire life. She'd be long gone before anything had a chance to happen between them.

Lucky for her. Lucky for both of them. Women and Weston and Wildacre just didn't mix.

She looked up at him, an expression of gratitude in her soft, stubborn gaze. "That's why I'll need your help. You can show me how to approach the animals."

There it was again, that hint of vulnerability in her voice. It had bothered her to ask him for that, bothered her to open up to him at all. Why? What was the lady trying to prove?

But even if he could read her, he was not the man to help her. Not with anything beyond the photo shoot, anyway. There were boundaries here, boundaries that were too dangerous for either of them to cross.

"I'm willing," he said. "But first, we need to get something straight. There are rules here that I expect you to obey, for the animals' safety as well as your own."

"I've worked under restricted conditions before," she told him, still a little defensive. "Just let me know what's off-limits. I'll do my best to respect your wishes."

His wishes? It was a good thing she didn't know what they were. He wished she wouldn't look at him like that, with so much challenge and defiance in the depths of those wide green eyes. He wished he hadn't noticed that soft sheath of brown silk hair, the way her face grew flushed when she was angry, the hint of pain she hid beneath that tough I-can-take-it exterior.

He wished he'd never laid eyes on the lady at all. He wished she'd get the hell out of there.

But as much as he'd like to, he couldn't just send her packing. Unfortunately, he had to let Ms. Eastbrook stick around for a while. He needed her. Or rather, his cats needed the article in *Eco* magazine. The publicity could go a long way to heighten public awareness of the endangered Florida panther. He'd spent years working for their cause, and this opportunity was too good to pass up.

The problem was, *she* came as part of the package deal. Lord help him, the next two weeks weren't going to be easy. He'd tell her what was off-limits, all right. He only hoped he'd remember himself.

"My bedroom," he said roughly.

"Excuse me?"

"My room," he amended, "is private. You're free to go anywhere else in the house. As for the grounds outside, don't try to explore on your own. The cats do have cages, but I only use them part-time. If you try to approach the animals without my supervision, I can't guarantee your safety."

She bit her lower lip, as if remembering the fear of meeting Fang for the first time, then nodded thoughtfully.

"Good," he said, picking up her bags with a kind of grim resignation. "Now come on. I'll show you to your room."

Faline followed him up the stairs to the second floor, where a series of doors opened off a wide hallway. Brand stood on the threshold of the second room, motioning her to enter. She stepped inside, charmed by the simple, uncluttered decor.

Panels of natural wood, neatly whitewashed, took on a soothing glow from the lighted ceiling fan above. On top of a plain dresser was a basket of enormous green pinecones softly scenting the air and the pale green bathroom beyond. A double bed stood alone in the corner, cool and inviting with a white embroidered quilt and creamy cotton sheets.

Faline decided the bedroom was relaxing, like a calm, peaceful paradise. At least it would have been if Brand wasn't in it. She watched as he deposited her bags at the base of the bed.

"Thanks."

He gave her a quick nod, said a brief good night, and in another moment he was gone.

Sighing thankfully, Faline dug a nightgown from the bottom of her suitcase, slipped it on, and snuggled gratefully between the sheets.

A purposeful tapping at her door woke Faline from a sound sleep. She bolted upright in bed, blinking at the bright morning light streaming in through the window shades.

"Yes?" she called out, pulling the sheets up to her neck. But the deep male voice she'd expected turned out to be a friendly female one instead.

"It's Mrs. Twitchford, dear. The housekeeper. May I come in?"

Relieved, and a little curious, Faline tumbled out of bed to answer the door. What kind of woman would be willing to look after the Wildman's home? Some nut, no doubt, as eccentric and antisocial as Weston himself.

But to her surprise, Mrs. Twitchford appeared to be entirely sane. No gleam of lunacy lit her kind gray eyes, no telltale hunch marred her sturdy figure. She was a robust healthy-looking woman, fifty-something and full of life.

She eyed Faline with an approving smile. "Well, what do you know? That boy's finally found himself a sweetheart brave enough to spend the night. You're not from around here, are you, honey?"

Faline shook her head vigorously and tried to set the woman straight. "Oh, it's not like that. I'm not anybody's sweetheart. I'm a photographer."

"Are you?" Mrs. Twitchford sounded doubtful, surveying the heavy camera bag, negative enlarger, and high-tech tripods with some suspicion. "Well, I'm just not sure about all that picture-taking," she said candidly. "I've had my photo done before, but it always made me feel odd, like I was sharing something too private." She lowered her voice an octave. "And there are some folks who still believe a camera can steal a person's soul."

Faline smiled inwardly at this frank, very open assessment of her work. It was refreshing, really. The locals weren't at all impressed by her artistic inclinations. But still, they were willing to give her a chance. On this ranch, at least, she'd have to prove herself all over again.

"I've heard that," she told the older woman. "Some primitive tribes believe that taking a person's picture will also take a part of him with it. I like to think of it another way—that I put a part of myself into every photo. I hope it will help even things out in the end."

Mrs. Twitchford nodded sagely, apparently agreeing with the logic. "Just be careful not to give away too much."

Faline suddenly wished she'd had this woman around many months ago, before she'd given away too much of herself to Scott. But even though he'd stolen her trust, her soul remained intact. And she had no intention of risking it again.

"Have you worked at the ranch very long?" Faline asked, as much out of curiosity as from a strong desire to change the subject.

The housekeeper patted the back of her no-nonsense hairdo, nodding thoughtfully. "Ever since the boy's mother took off," she said.

Faline's eyebrows went up a notch as she realized that "the boy" must be Brand. Not exactly the term she'd use to describe him, but apparently Mrs. Twitchford still saw him as a youngster.

"Took off?" Faline asked. "You mean she abandoned him?"

Mrs. Twitchford nodded, her lips tightening. "Left the boy when he was only six. Can you imagine? Deserted the husband too. Claimed she couldn't take the ranch anymore. Too much isolation and boredom."

Faline felt her heart constricting in sympathy for "the boy," and her mind wandered back over their conversation the night before. The fiancée he'd mentioned—Katrina. She'd left the ranch as well. It seemed there was a pattern of desertion in the Wildman's past. The women he'd loved had a habit of leaving. Was that what had made him so determined to survive on his own?

But it wasn't any of her business, really. And by all appearances, the grown-up Mr. Weston could take care of himself just fine.

"At least he had his father," Faline suggested,

feeling a little uncomfortable over the personal nature of the conversation.

But it didn't seem to bother Mrs. T. one bit. It'd probably been a long time since she'd had anyone to discuss the subject with. She warmed to it, walking to the windows, slowly drawing back the blinds.

"The father was a changed man after the wife left. Put all of himself into this land. Turned it into one of the biggest cattle ranches around. Only trouble was, he had nothing left to give to his son."

Faline felt that same compassionate tug inside her again. At least she'd been lucky enough to have both parents. Brand apparently hadn't had anyone to depend on. No one except himself.

She wasn't sure what to say. "Didn't Brand inherit the ranch?" she asked.

Mrs. Twitchford nodded. "Oh, the father left him well-off, all right. Half the land's leased to citrus growers now, brings in a good income. But I wasn't talking about money."

Faline fell silent for a moment, trying to imagine a young boy growing up with no parental concern or supervision, as undomesticated as the animals in the overgrown forest outside. Other than school, he'd been used to isolation all his life. He hadn't had any choice.

"Lucky he had you to help raise him," she murmured to Mrs. T.

A soft smile lit the housekeeper's face, giving her a beauty acquired from years of living, as deep and mysterious as the finish on a fine antique vase. "Lucky for me," she insisted. "And I'm not sure I did so much. Brand's always been a loner. Preferred the company of animals to anyone else. And who can blame him? It's not his fault he grew up half wild."

Fascinated in spite of herself, Faline couldn't help inquiring further. "Half wild? So he's always been that way?"

Mrs. Twitchford dusted the top of the dresser with a rag and carefully rearranged the pinecone basket. "That boy's had a gift with wild things ever since he was a baby. Started bringing lizards in the house at first. After that it was a hawk he'd found with an injured wing. Tamed it like the princes do in those fairy tales, making it fly off to do his bidding."

She paused for a moment and shuddered. "Next thing I knew, he'd saved a bobcat from his father's shotgun. I guess it'd been hungry, kept looking for food closer to the ranch and made the cattle skittish. But Brand wouldn't let the old man harm it. Wanted me to let it sleep with him in his room! Imagine that."

Faline *was* imagining, but somehow the idea of Brand sleeping with an untamed bobcat didn't sound the least bit unusual.

"Did you let him?" she asked, smiling.

Mrs. Twitchford gave her a horrified stare. "Lord, no!" she exclaimed. "I draw the line at clawing critters." She sniffed defensively. "Besides, that was the day I decided I was allergic to cats. Especially the big ones."

Faline grinned. "So you're not too fond of tigers?"

"Fond of 'em?" Mrs. Twitchford scoffed. "I just don't want them to get too fond of me. I haven't set foot in that yard for over ten years. Not since he turned a perfectly good cattle ranch into this lethal lion's den. I drive here in my car every morning, and I leave in my car every evening, and that's the way I like it."

Faline hopefully considered the possibility of photographing the cats from the safety of an automobile, then remembered the provoking remarks Weston had made about the Jeep tour and discarded the idea with regret. It was too restrictive, anyway. Sooner or later, she'd have to face them, claws, fangs, and all. Sooner or later she'd have to face *him* again. It was hard to decide which she dreaded more.

"Where's Mr. Weston?" she asked as casually as she could manage.

"Out with the animals," Mrs. T. explained, walking to the door. "But I'll be serving breakfast in twenty minutes. You can see him there," she added, winking.

Faline ignored the suggestion in the older woman's voice. Could she help it if Mrs. Twitchford had the wrong idea about her and Brand? It would soon be obvious that her interest in "the boy" was purely professional. Besides, anyone could see they were completely mismatched. The only *sweetheart* suitable for the Wildman would be a submissive, stringy-haired cavewoman, tough as a Florida gator, and willing to swing from the trees.

"I'll be down as soon as I get dressed," she promised, then turned her attention on what to wear.

A suit of armor would be the most appropriate outfit for the occasion, but she didn't happen to have one handy in her suitcase. She opted for a pair of simple white shorts instead, with a formfitting lightweight T-shirt she'd picked up for her trip. But as soon as she found her way into the kitchen and felt Brand slowly inspecting her with those all-seeing eyes, she began to regret the decision.

His amber-gold gaze raked across the thin blue shirt with an interest that was almost involuntary. It reminded Faline of the stare the tiger had turned on her. It was curious, intense, territorial. She fought the urge to run back upstairs and add several more layers to the outfit.

"Good morning," she managed to say calmly. "Ready to get to work?"

Work? Brand repeated to his distracted brain. Who was she kidding? From the sleek, sensual look of her, the next two weeks were going to be a lot more difficult than he'd imagined.

Even harder to ignore was the gleam of determination in her eyes. He'd never met a woman with so much outward mettle and so many internal defenses. She wouldn't admit to fear for anything. She was ready to get on with it.

Well, *he* was ready to get it over with, to get her out of there. But he couldn't help wondering what would happen if she ever let her guard down. Couldn't help wondering what kind of persuasion it would take to help her do it. Couldn't help calling himself a fool for even considering the idea.

"We'll start after breakfast," he answered gruffly, holding out a chair for her at the kitchen counter.

She ate her morning meal eagerly, adapting herself to the strange surroundings, enjoying his housekeeper's country cooking with unreserved pleasure. *Not a bit shy,* Brand observed.

"Delicious," she said, bestowing an appreciative smile on Mrs. Twitchford.

Brand hadn't even touched his food. In fact, he'd hardly noticed it.

"Lost your appetite?" Mrs. Twitchford asked in concern. "Because it isn't like you to pass up a meal," she added.

No, Brand agreed silently. It wasn't like him at all. And it wasn't like him to be so disturbed by a stray Wildcat in woman's clothing. He'd met up with provoking creatures before, but something told him Ms. Eastbrook was going to be his greatest challenge.

She was a woman he couldn't help responding

to. A woman who needed to let go. And he was a man who could show her how.

Paws off, he told himself firmly, as though issuing a crucial command to Fang. The lady would only be staying for a short while, and that was ample reason to leave her alone.

"I'm fine," he assured his loyal housekeeper, pushing the plate away with his apologies. He turned to Faline. "You'll need to see the rest of the ranch." His voice was even and matter-of-fact. "But you'd better put something on." *Like a nun's habit*, he added silently.

Faline wrinkled her brow at him, polishing off the last of the crumbs on her plate. "Put something on?"

He sighed inwardly with pent-up frustration. Didn't she realize the effect she was having on him? Didn't she know she was the first single woman to set foot on his property in a very long time?

Last night it hadn't been quite so bad. Last night it'd been dark. And she'd been dressed. In a blouse, long skirt, and stockings, at least. Last night she'd looked far too scared and vulnerable to make love to.

This morning, she'd gotten her bearings. Now *he* was the one who was hurting.

"The woods out there are full of bloodthirsty creatures," he explained. "Insects that like to feed on bare arms and legs."

"Oh," she said in understanding. "Don't worry, I brought my repellent along."

Brand gave her another once-over and slowly shook his head. "I don't think it's going to be strong enough."

She widened her eyes at him. "Really? They must be pretty bad in this area."

Brand nodded, his voice a little hoarse. "Ruthless. Very determined."

Faline shrugged. "I brought some jeans and a long-sleeved shirt. Will those do?"

Brand inclined his head. They'd have to.

But as soon as she'd changed and met him at the door, he wondered if there was any improvement at all. The jeans were what he'd call a perfect fit, and the white blouse was far too clingy for his comfort.

"Ready?" he asked.

She nodded grimly and slung the camera strap over her shoulder.

THREE

As soon as they'd stepped outside, Faline took a careful, cautious glance around. She couldn't see any wild beasts in the near vicinity, but with Tarzan in charge, anything was possible.

"Hey, Weston," she called after him, "are all the kitties safely in their cages?"

He stopped and turned toward her, nodding impatiently. "It's morning mealtime. They eat in separate runs so the food is distributed fairly. Now, are you going to come down off that porch or do I have to carry you?"

"I can walk just fine without your help, thank you." She tiptoed slowly down the steps and added hopefully, "That tiger I saw yesterday, what was his name—Fang? Yes, Fang. I suppose he's locked up too?"

Brand gave her a quick half grin. "Don't worry. He's feeding."

Faline let out a long sigh of relief, hurried down the stairs, and did her best to keep up with the Wildman's long, easy strides. "So what do tigers eat, anyway?" She was almost panting from the effort to match his pace.

Brand took a turn onto a narrow path leading to the thickest part of the forest, walking ahead of her single file. He shot her a cursory glance over his shoulder. "Protein, mainly. They're carnivores."

Don't remind me, she thought, suddenly wishing she'd picked another subject. "I don't suppose they make a tiger chow, do they? I mean, surely you don't feed them anything . . . *live?*" she asked in morbid fascination.

"Like pesky photographers, you mean?"

She shook her head, clinging to her jostling camera with one arm and trying to maintain her balance with the other. "No, like"—she could hardly bear to think of it—"like little creatures."

"I never feed them anything cute, cuddly, or still squirming. Guess that leaves you out," he added gravely.

Before Faline could decide which category he meant to fit her in, he continued. "We keep all the cats on a diet of grocery meat and vitamins. The local vet makes sure it's nutritionally balanced."

They finally reached a clearing in the woods where an enormous wire cage, nearly as big as her own apartment, nestled among the trees. "Take a look," Brand suggested. "I think you'll agree the food keeps them strong and healthy."

Faline followed his gaze beyond the protective wire to a group of smooth sandstone boulders. On the highest rock, a magnificent male lion was sunning himself with paws outstretched, his wise feline eyes focused on the harem below. The three lionesses he guarded were slightly smaller, but no less impressive as they hissed and spat at one another, vying for position on a favorite patch of ground.

Faline cautiously approached the cage, and let out a small, involuntary gasp. She'd never gotten so close to such animals even when she'd visited the zoo, and at this proximity they were far more beautiful than she'd imagined. Their soft fur glistened in the sun like molten gold, their lithe muscles rippling beneath. Their eyes were an eerie, improbable yellow, glimmering and mysterious. *Marvelous*, she thought. *Very exotic. And very scary.*

"This group is East-African," Brand explained, "zoo bred. But the zoo went under for lack of funds and there was no place to house them. This ranch was their last refuge."

Faline couldn't take her eyes off the incredible cats. "But couldn't they be set free? Taken back to Africa?" she asked hopefully.

Brand shook his head, eyeing the animals with grim resolution. "Unfortunately not. This bunch is too domesticated by now. They'd starve to death in the wild. Or worse."

Faline's heart went out to the stranded animals, but before she had a chance to reply, the female closest to the cage took a sudden dislike to their new visitor. The lioness unexpectedly leapt up from a crouching position and lunged at Faline, swatting at the inner wires with her giant paw. Faline jumped back and found herself clinging to Brand's T-shirt, cradled protectively in the strong circle of his arms.

"Easy," he said in a low voice that was infinitely calm, infinitely soothing. But Faline wasn't sure if he was addressing her or the irritated animal.

The female cat responded to his soft command and backed away from the wires to resume her position on the ground, but she continued to watch them with wide, wary eyes. Faline reacted to Brand's voice as well, but his sensual tone, combined with the intimate way he was holding her, brought her excitement level up instead of down.

"Relax." His voice sent shivers down her spine. "You can't run away now. She'll only sense your fear."

"I'm not afraid," she insisted foolishly. *Not afraid of the cat*, she amended silently.

Brand laughed softly and held one hand at the tender base of her throat, feeling the fluttering pulse beneath her bare skin. "Oh no?" he asked quietly, his breath erotically tickling against her ear. "So why is your heart beating so fast? It's part of the flight or fight response, a natural adrenaline-producing reaction to danger. You have a choice now, either to run or stand your ground. Which will it be?"

Faline felt the adrenaline rushing through her body all right, but the fear strangely intensified her awareness of him. The touch, the smell, the feel of the Wildman were all powerfully amplified by her body's sudden chemical surge. And she wasn't at all sure how to handle the new, unexpected sensation.

"I'm not going anywhere, if that's what you mean," she said testily. *Not until I can move again.*

Brand didn't let go, but turned her around to meet his intense amber gaze. "A good choice," he told her. "There's nothing more tempting to a predator than a quarry who decides to run. The thrill of a good chase is almost irresistible."

And man, Faline remembered from freshman biology class, was the fiercest creature of all. From the sharks in the ocean to the tigers in the forest, no animal on earth was more dangerous.

She put one hand on her camera and shrugged her way out of his arms. "I've had some experience with *predators,*" she told him. "Met up with my share of them back in the big city. It'll take more than that to make me run."

Brand gave a slow grin and led her away from the lion pride to the next cage in the woods. Fang was there, all four hundred pounds of him, but behind the safety of the bars he looked a little less ferocious than she remembered. The beach ball he was playing with might've had something to do with her revised impression. He looked a lot like an overgrown frisky house cat, chasing after a giant kitty toy.

Brand called out to him as they approached, in a gruff voice that couldn't hide his obvious affection for the animal. The tiger's ears pricked forward when the Wildman called his name, and he abandoned the ball for the anticipated treat of a visit from his master. Fang bounded eagerly toward the bars, lifted himself up on two paws, and nuzzled his head against the cage.

Faline watched in amazement as Brand responded to the tiger's gesture, sticking his arm precariously between the wires and rubbing him roughly on the head and neck, scratching him hard behind the ears. Fang gave his master a look of sheer adoration before his eyes rolled blissfully back in his head. Faline marveled at the complete trust between them.

"You remember Fang," Brand said, turning to give her one of those heart-stopping half smiles.

"Vaguely," she answered, smiling back. But the tiger and his owner were both unforgettable. "I guess you two like each other."

He nodded, still stroking the ecstatic animal behind the ears. "I guess you could say that. Fang's a four-year-old Bengal tiger. Unfortunately, the previous owners had him declawed when he was a cub, then decided they really didn't want him after all. He wasn't fit for much after that. It's taken some time, but the ranch here seems to suit him pretty well. He's finally learned to trust me."

Faline eyed the big cat from a distance, but didn't attempt to approach the cage. "Trust a man?" she asked doubtfully. "Now, there's a concept. Can't say I blame old Fang for taking his time."

Brand felt the tension in her words and frowned. "It may be a slow process," he said, "but no one can build a decent relationship without trust. Man or animal."

"Oh I believe you," Faline said. "Theoretically. But in practice?" She shrugged. "Let's just say it hasn't worked for me."

It was the catch in her voice that stirred his compassion, the hint of bitterness that lay beneath. Brand wondered who it was that had hurt her and how much experience Ms. Eastbrook had had with men. Not a lot, he imagined. For all her tough-acting exterior, he sensed that she was really sweet inside. A nice lady. Not entirely innocent, but still a little wet behind the ears. Sensitive. Susceptible.

The kind of woman who could bring out a man's most powerful protective instincts. And some of the more primitive ones as well.

"Trust isn't something a man takes from you, Faline. It's something he's supposed to earn."

She looked away, and the sun caught the moisture in her eyes. "Tell that to my ex-business partner," she suggested.

"Your partner? Is he the one who did this to

you?" Brand knew the answer before she'd spoken it.

She gave him a wry smile. "You know what they say about mixing business with pleasure? Well, I didn't listen."

Brand didn't have to ask if the relationship had gone wrong. It was clear that some slime bag had hurt her. Much more than she seemed willing to admit. He let his hands drop to his sides, reflexively clenching his fingers into fists.

Fang let out a low growl of protest when the scratching stopped. He tapped his head gently against the cage, reminding Brand to keep up the action behind the ears.

Faline laughed, and Brand reached inside the cage again to comfort the tiger. "Too bad that guy was already an ex-partner when this assignment came up," he commented dryly. "If he'd showed up here, Fang would've made mincemeat out of him."

She smiled. "As appealing as that idea is, I'm glad he didn't come along. I needed the job myself."

She'd needed it. Brand warned himself not to forget that very important fact. She was here to do a job, nothing more. What other reason was there for a woman to come to Wildacre? What other reason to stay? "Of course."

"I'm glad I took it," she added earnestly. "It's an interesting place to visit."

"Uh-huh," he responded. *But you wouldn't want to live here.*

Faline focused her attention on the tiger, on the interaction between the big cat and Brand. It was remarkable to watch the way the man and beast were bonding. It almost made her a bit envious to see the closeness between them.

What would it feel like, she wondered, to have the Wildman touch her in that caring, caressing way? How could a man be so tender and tough at the same time? How could she even let herself *think* about it?

"He seems a little friendlier than the lions," she observed, trying to keep her eyes on the animal.

Brand nodded. "Fang's in training to be an animal actor—he's still learning to tolerate people."

"Still learning?" Faline asked warily. "You mean he hasn't passed the course yet?"

A wry smile tilted the corners of his mouth. "Fang's still a bit skittish around strangers. The film studios in Orlando have hired us a few times, but only for small parts where principal actors weren't involved. They can't afford to risk their investment."

"Oh great!" she responded in mock relief. "I feel so much better now. I suppose Fang doesn't have as much appetite for mere photographers."

Brand's gaze swiftly raked the length of her body in speculation. "I suppose you'd do as an hors d'oeuvre."

"Barbarian," she shot back smoothly, but her face was flushed.

He finally let go of Fang and leaned against the cage, continuing to observe her as he flicked back his long golden ponytail and casually crossed his arms.

The Beastmaster, Faline thought. Cocky. Unafraid. A man with the sort of inborn bravado that women found irresistible. Probably had to chase them back with a whip.

"Ready for the rest of the tour?" he asked.

She followed him expectantly past the last few cages, stopping at the end to observe a tan, white-whiskered feline, somewhat smaller than Fang and the lions.

"A mountain lion?" she asked, unsure of the species.

"Close. A Florida panther. The coloring's nearly identical."

"She's lovely," Faline sighed, intrigued by this sleek, strangely elegant animal.

At the sound of her voice, the panther shifted her position in the cage, stretched a bit, and struggled to a standing position. A small, lightly spotted cub, who'd apparently been nursing at his mother's side, suddenly came into view.

"A kitten! He's adorable!"

Brand led her up to the cage for a closer look. "Take it slow," he cautioned, grabbing her unceremoniously by the back of her shirt collar and checking her forward progress. "Mama's notoriously protective."

The panther took a few steps toward them in curiosity, and Faline noticed a slight limp in her stride, as though her back leg had been injured or broken. "Is she hurt?"

"Car accident," Brand replied bluntly. "Some damn fool hit her and left her by the side of the road to die."

Faline understood the anger in his tone. How could anyone harm such an exquisite animal? And even if it had been an accident, how could they simply desert her on the highway? "Where did it happen?"

Still holding her by the shirt, Brand raked his spare hand thoughtfully across his jaw, barely keeping his anger in check. "Their natural range is several hours south of here, in the Everglades area. A ranger discovered her and the cub, and the Panther Interagency Committee brought them here to recuperate. Another week or two and they should be well enough to set free again."

Faline watched, enchanted, as the kitten took a few stumbling steps forward, swatted fiercely at a dragonfly, then tripped over his own tail. Reflexively, she reached for her camera, snapping a few shots of the little charmer and his not-so-frisky mother. The cage posed something of an aesthetic problem, but she wasn't ready to step inside yet. She'd capture the next part of the story when the panthers were released into the wild.

Brand let go of her collar when she started shooting and stood back to let her do her thing. The lady seemed to know her business, and he didn't intend to interfere unless things got rough. But the cat showed no signs of stress, and Faline showed every sign of enjoying herself. In fact, he was extremely pleased that she'd found his panthers so fascinating.

Her appreciation for the cats would make the photos turn out that much better. *His* appreciation was focused on something else.

He liked the way she moved, twisting and turning to find just the right angle. Dedication, that's what the lady had. Determination. Not to mention some very interesting angles of her own. He'd never realized before just how fascinating photography could be.

"That's the last of this film. Mind if I start another roll?"

"No problem."

She leaned a little to one side, still peering through the camera at the panthers. "I appreciate your cooperation," she told him. "It's really a big help."

He didn't take his eyes off her, drawn in by her obvious love for her work, mesmerized by her movements. "You're doing just fine without me."

"After all," she said, sliding her legs a little apart, shifting her weight forward as the shutter release continued clicking at top speed, "we both want the same thing."

Do we?

She stopped for a moment, turning to smile up at him, an enticing sparkle of fervency lit her expression. Pleasure, excitement? He couldn't tell, but her skin was flushed from the morning heat, and damp tendrils of her smooth brown hair had escaped to curl softly at her temples.

She looked beautiful crouching there, and a little afraid of him, too, clutching her precious camera in hand, as though she half-believed he would take it away from her.

But the camera didn't concern him one bit. What did worry him was the way she looked at him, the way her emerald eyes flashed fear and hurt and hope in the space of a single glance. Desire surged within him suddenly, sweet and sharp. The desire to make all her hurt go away. The desire to replace her pain with something far more pleasurable.

He longed to help her in the only way he knew how. Physically, instinctively, without words. He longed to touch her in the most intimate way imaginable. To soothe her body with his until she was flat on her back beneath him.

He longed to let her go. Now. To *make* her leave before nature could take its course. Because if he did take her to bed, Brand knew he'd pay in the end.

Sooner or later she'd be bolting back to the civilized world. The same way Katrina had, that summer he'd brought her home to his ranch from college. She'd promised to marry him, to live with him at Wildacre forever. But to Katrina, forever had meant two months.

She'd didn't like the seclusion, couldn't imagine being buried on some cattle ranch for the rest of her life. She'd given him back his ring, his affection, and his freedom.

A lot like his loyal, loving mother had so many years before. At least Mom had stuck around the first six years of his life. Just long enough to let him get attached. Long enough to teach him what good-byes were all about.

But he was a man now. He'd learned to keep things casual. Some women, he'd discovered, were willing to make meaningful relationships in the course of a few hours. And Brand had been willing to get meaningful right back. A man had his physical needs, after all.

But something told him that Faline was the kind of lady who'd expect more. She'd clearly been burned pretty bad in the past. Mistreated to the point where she was afraid to trust. It would take a lot to make her come around, maybe more than he had to give.

Besides, he wasn't a complete barbarian, no matter what she'd called him. He could keep himself in check for two weeks if necessary. And with a downright dangerous, desirable lady like Faline around, some serious restraint on his part would be very necessary.

"Meet you at the house?" he asked, deciding his tortured brain and body had had enough.

"You're not leaving me alone!"

"The wires are strong. The cats won't get out."

She glanced uneasily over her shoulder, at the long row of cages, and shuddered slightly, standing to sling the camera strap over her shoulder. "No way, Weston, I'm coming with you."

"Suit yourself." He shrugged, and led her back through the forest.

Faline's eyes gradually adjusted to the dim reddish light of her new makeshift darkroom. Mrs. Twitchford had been kind enough to clear out a walk-in linen closet for her use, and Faline had spent most of the afternoon mixing chemicals, preparing to develop the morning's film. She'd just loaded the second roll in her canister and was trying to print a contact sheet on the first, when Brand knocked on the door.

"Wildcat? What the hell are you doing in the closet?"

She wasn't sure exactly how to explain. She finished counting the exposure time on her nightglow watch and cracked the door a few inches. "Hurry up and get inside. I'll show you."

But as soon as Brand had stepped over the threshold and shut the door behind him, Faline realized her mistake. The closet wasn't big enough for the both of them. Weston's body took up too much room.

She could hardly move without rubbing against some part of him, whether it was those wide shoulders, the incredibly tight waist, or the long, powerful legs. She swallowed air, finding it difficult to breathe.

"I'm printing up a proof sheet on those shots I took earlier," she explained, summoning up the most professional tone she could manage. "This way I can check exposures, study the composition, and look for any other problems."

Brand's eyes raked the length of her body in the semidarkness. "Problems?" he asked softly. "Do you think we might have any?"

She turned back to agitate the vat of chemical developer, wondering how to respond. She had a problem, all right, but it wasn't necessarily with the work. Did he sense it, too, the tension that was building between them? Or was it just her imagination working overtime again?

"Not that I'm aware of," she lied. But what else could she say? She couldn't confess just how aware of him she was at the moment. She could barely admit it to herself.

"It's hot in here," she murmured, trying to edge herself into a less awkward position. Her back was to him, but she could feel the entire length of his body against her. Waist, thighs, everything.

"It's gonna get a hell of a lot hotter if you don't stop doing that."

"Doing what? I was only trying to give you more room."

"Quit *wiggling*," he said, grabbing her waist with both hands. "Now hold still before you get yourself into trouble and give me something else by mistake. This space is tight enough already."

"Oh!" she said, shocked into silence. He was talking about an erection of course. It wasn't like she'd never seen one before. But a fully aroused wildman was an entirely different creature from a politely excited, well-mannered urban male.

Scott had always apologized for any sexual performance that bordered on the unrefined. Brand would likely drag her off by her hair and boldly subject her to fierce, remorseless animal lust. It stunned her to realize she'd far prefer the Wildman's methods. At least his intentions would be honest.

But as fascinating as the thought was, Faline didn't intend to experience any of Weston's techniques, sexual or otherwise. It wasn't that she was afraid of him—okay, so maybe she was a little afraid. Entrusting her body to a man like Weston was out of the question. Savages were not acceptable companions for city girls. Scarier still was the idea of risking her soul.

She wasn't about to make that mistake again. Especially with a man so undomesticated and unpredictable. With a man so bold and independent, so break-your-heart handsome, he was bound to leave her with some kind of emotional scars. And

Lord knew, she had enough of those to last a very long time.

Brand's body jostled her back to reality. He was trying to extricate himself from a very precarious position, shifting slowly behind her, but there was very little to hold on to in the tiny room. His hands had started to stray where they didn't belong.

"Do you *mind*? That's not my shoulder you're grabbing there, buddy."

Brand jerked his hand away and swore violently into the darkness. "Calm down, will you? I'm not going to attack you in a closet. There's not enough room."

She stiffened slightly, crossing her arms in front of her, but the protective move only drew a laugh of amusement from him.

"Are all you big-town women this uptight?"

She lifted her chin a little and turned to give him an icy stare. "Only around rustic cavemen. I'll thank you to keep your hands to yourself."

"Sure thing. But you might thank me more if I didn't."

She flushed hotly, grateful for the cloak of darkness around them. Maybe she really did want him to touch her. She'd been thinking about it earlier, hadn't she? Had he read it in her eyes, sensed it in the same way he gauged the tiger's mood?

She was attracted to him, heaven help her. But her fascination went far beyond the physical. There was another side to this man that made her want to move closer. The side that could calm tigers with the sound of his voice. The side that took in homeless lions and protected vulnerable panther cubs. The intensely private side he never showed to the rest of the world.

"Hey," he said, tugging on a stray lock of her hair, "what about the pictures?"

The contact sheet! She'd almost forgotten. She turned it over in the developer bath, and peered down into the clear liquid for a first look at her photos. Brand towered over her, leaning too close for comfort as he craned for a better view.

"Not bad," he commented generously.

Not bad? Some compliment, Faline thought wryly, carefully transferring the proof sheet to the stop bath. He'd sure passed judgment on her work pretty quick. Just who did he think he was?

But then she took a closer look at the photos and realized with illogical irritation that he was right. *Not bad* was the nicest thing she could find to say about them herself. The pictures definitely weren't up to par.

"Did you say something?" he prompted.

Vail would've taken one look and tossed the whole batch into the trash. But Brand had the nerve to be nice about it. Didn't he realize she could do better? A little stung, she said dryly, "I'll get it right next time."

He hooked his fingers in the back of her jeans, pulling her around to face him. "It's no use. You'd like to claw my eyes out, wouldn't you? Go ahead and try."

"Don't be ridiculous." She pretended to study the dial of her watch, hoping that he couldn't hear the hard pounding of her heart. "I'm just a little disappointed in the photos. My work is usually better than that."

He tucked a hand under her chin and tilted her face up to meet his. "I think we both know the reason, don't we?"

Faline's heart was beating wildly now. Those eyes seemed to penetrate the very depths of her soul, reminding her that the Wildman had a way of reading other creature's minds. He'd guessed how she felt about him. He *knew* what she'd been thinking.

"You're afraid," he continued, not waiting for an answer.

Faline swallowed hard, but there was no denying it. Her adrenaline glands had been working overtime from her first minute on Wildacre Ranch. Brand Weston scared the hell out of her.

"You've got to get over it," he said bluntly. "You'll never get a decent photo until you're on the other side of that cage. This isn't going to work until you overcome your fear of the animals."

Faline blinked up at him. The animals? Of course she was afraid of man-eating, no, *woman*-eating cats. Who wouldn't be? But Brand was quickly becoming the primary distraction. Her only relief was the fact that he didn't seem to realize it.

"Any suggestions?" she asked faintly.

"A few." He impulsively stroked the side of her face with his hand. "Loosen up a little. Relax. The cats can sense when you're nervous."

Lord, but her face was soft, Brand decided, just like the rest of her. Soft and sweet and warm, like a kitten, cuddling up next to him. A kitten who wanted to be touched.

He watched her close her eyes, letting go just a little, and Brand felt a hard catch of desire inside. This was the part of her he'd known was there all along. The vulnerable part that needed to trust again. The part he wanted to make completely his.

He put his arm out and eased her closer, swearing softly when her body relaxed against his. He knew she was trying to please him, responding to his wishes, to his command. Hell, did she have to pick now to quit fighting him and go all soft and sweet?

After so many months of deprivation, the temptation to gentle her was too great. It'd been too damn long since he'd held a woman in his arms, especially one so incredibly responsive. He had only to move his hand a little, to shift his weight just so, and she reacted instantly.

He brushed his hand across the downy surface of her neck, testing, and drew a shiver of excitement from her. She was with him every step of the way. He tilted her head back, and watched her eyes flutter open, a flashing mirror of his own painful desire. He had to taste her, just this once, and to hell with the consequences. He bent his head to kiss her.

FOUR

Inches away from the warm promise of her mouth, Brand checked himself, and drew back. He watched Faline's eyes open wider, a little unsure, a little afraid, but willing to let him try. It was that "don't hurt me" look in her eyes that stopped him, that he wasn't sure he could handle.

Something in his gut squeezed and tightened. She was even more susceptible than he'd imagined. Too vulnerable to take so soon.

Faline was a creature out of her environment, a woman who'd wandered into territory where she didn't belong. *His* territory. The lady didn't realize what she was getting herself into. But he did. And it was a situation neither of them was ready for.

"Is something wrong?" she whispered, those liquid green eyes locked with his.

Hell yes, there was something wrong. He'd nearly lost it for a minute there, nearly gotten them both in over their heads. She wasn't near ready to trust again. He doubted he'd ever be ready to help her try.

What was it about this particular female that made him hold back, waiting for the moment when she was fully aware of her own actions? What was it about her that warned him to stay away?

He released her abruptly, gesturing to the enlarger and the liquid-filled trays of developing solution. "The chemicals must be getting to me. I'd better get out of here."

Faline felt the disappointment as palpably as an aching physical pain, centered deep within her. When Brand pulled away so suddenly, it seemed as though her breath had caught low in her belly and settled there, waiting for him to set it free. And then, inexplicably, he'd let her go.

She fought the urge to reach out and pull him back, to give in to the physical ache, the sheer primal need of a man, *this* man. But she couldn't abandon herself so completely.

She couldn't believe she'd left herself so wide open. Not to a man she'd met only recently. Not to a man she'd be leaving all too soon.

She spent the remainder of the afternoon in the familiar cloak of the darkroom, the pungent smell of the solutions, the slick feel of the photographic paper, the hard edges of the enlarger bringing her a well-known comfort and temporary peace. She was at home among these things as nowhere else, and drew security from them.

A security that was lost as soon as she saw Brand again, across the dinner table, with the evening twilight visible through the windows at his back. Two bug-fighting citronella candles graced the centerpiece, apparently Mrs. Twitchford's idea of setting a romantic mood. But the flickering lights that played across Brand's face gave his bronzed features a surrealistic look, as though his high, burnished cheekbones and angular jaw had been cast in sleek molten metal.

He stood when she approached and gestured to the chair opposite him. It was strange to see him exhibiting such unexpected gallantry toward her. The primal power of the man gave his actions even greater meaning. He'd stood because he wished to, as a sign of respect, not out of habit like Scott. Weston's intent added intimacy to the moment, as though he'd acknowledged his superior strength and relinquished it to her in one smooth movement of his body.

She nodded and sat without speaking, wishing he didn't look quite so magnificent. If only he'd do something crass and boorish, like toss a bone across the table to her, she might feel a little more at ease. But there was no coarseness in the way he poured the chilled wine, handing her a shimmering, moist glass.

It was sweet to the taste, and Faline took several generous sips, hoping it would give her the courage to face the evening ahead. "Nice," she acknowledged. "The flavor's unusual."

"A honey-wine," he told her. "The fermenting process is centuries old, but we make our own here, thanks to the local bees and orange blossoms."

Faline took another sip, musing how appropriate it seemed for Brand to be brewing the ancient liqueur. The same self-sufficient way his ancestors probably had so many years ago.

He set his own glass on the table, leaning forward. "Tomorrow we can try a few shots without the cage—if you think you're ready."

She nodded, a wry smile on her lips. "I know *I'm* ready. It's the animals I'm worried about. Too bad we can't ask them what they'd like. 'Pardon me, Fang. Will you be having the usual today, or perhaps you'd prefer some fresh photographer, just flown in from New York?' "

Brand grinned in appreciation, his teeth flashing white in the candlelight. "It's unlikely that Fang would order you off a menu. Chicken necks are his favorite food."

"Chicken necks?" she asked, glancing doubtfully down at her plate.

Brand shook his head reassuringly. "Baked bluefish. If I fed you chicken tonight, it could mean trouble tomorrow. Anything that smells even faintly of poultry is fair game to Fang, and in serious danger of being devoured."

Faline watched the candle fire play across his sensual, almost savage features, his eyes glowing amber in the gathering dark.

"But the neck is Fang's favorite part?" she asked, curious.

"The cartilage helps to keep his teeth clean. He gets his fill of chicken five days a week, along with the regular meat diet and some vitamin supplements. That's about as close as we can come to the natural feeding habits of a Bengal tiger."

"Only five days a week? Doesn't he want to eat every day?"

Brand gave her a speculative stare. "Sometimes what we want isn't the same as what's good for us."

Faline didn't miss the double meaning in his words. Was this his way of explaining what had happened between them earlier? And he was right, wasn't he? The risks here were too high for her to give in to her feelings. Letting go like that was completely out of the question. At least it was for her.

"And what do you want?" she asked softly.

His eyes blazed in the firelight, reminding her forcefully of a poem she'd studied at school. *Tyger, tyger, burning bright . . .*

He took a long sip of wine and sat back, twirling the glass gently between his fingertips. "Chicken necks are a true temptation to Fang. He'd eat them all day if I let him, but it's much healthier to feed him in measured doses. Healthier and *safer*. As for me . . ." He paused, watching her.

"As for you," she prompted, running her finger lightly around the rim of her own glass, raising it to wet her lips with the drops of wine gathered there. She stopped, out of breath at the expression she read in his eyes.

"When I get a taste of something I like," his voice was a low, warning whisper, "I'm not willing to settle for a single portion. Even though too much of a good thing can be—dangerous."

The message seemed clear enough. He was telling her to proceed at her own risk. Warning her that once certain lines were crossed there would be no going back. For either of them. She gripped her own glass tightly. "So when is the pleasure worth the risk?"

He smiled slowly. "That's something you have to decide for yourself."

Mrs. Twitchford bustled in, breaking the tension, removing their half-empty plates. "Anyone who wants coffee, better speak now. It's near dark already, and I'm not hanging around when those creatures outside start screeching and caterwaulin' like banshees. Gives me the shivers for sure, and Doc Ryder agrees that shivers are no good. Besides, if those lions start growling again, it might just aggravate my allergies."

Faline met Brand's eyes across the table and smiled. At least the Wildman had a sense of humor. And he treated Mrs. T. with the sort of patience and kindness the loyal lady deserved. His eyes kindled with amused tolerance when he spoke.

"Good night," he told the harried housekeeper, and thanked her.

Faline added her own gratitude and grinned as Mrs. Twitchford made a shuddering exit, shutting the dining room door behind her.

Faline leaned forward. "Doc Ryder?" she whispered in curiosity.

"A buddy of mine," he explained. "With the world's smoothest bedside manner. He 'treats' her allergies with a sympathetic ear, and usually leaves this house with a car full of baked goods, and half the food from my freezer."

"A physician who makes house calls?" she asked in surprise. "Not many New York doctors are willing to do that. Your Mrs. Twitchford is a fortunate patient."

He laughed softly. "The doctors are the same in Winter Haven as they are in New York, Faline. You see, Twitchford isn't really one of Marshall's patients, and 'Doc Ryder' isn't exactly a physician. He's a vet."

"A vet! Your customs here could take a lot of getting used to."

The smile left his eyes. "It isn't the big city. Some people never adjust to the isolation."

Faline blinked in surprise, a little taken aback by the bluntness of his reaction. She hadn't meant to open an old wound, and she felt a sudden urge to comfort him. An odd reaction, she knew. Brand was a big, brawny tiger trainer. Fierce, ferocious, and fearless. He didn't need her understanding. He didn't need anything from her at all.

"The town itself isn't so isolated," she finally responded. "I passed plenty of homes and businesses on my way from the airport. As for your ranch—"

"My ranch is, shall we say—secluded. And the town's been built up a lot in the last twenty years. It used to be no more than a bump in the road. I can still remember my mother complaining . . ." He let his voice trail away, reluctant to continue.

"She didn't like it here?" Faline prompted.

He gave a low, bitter laugh. "Didn't like anything about the place. Not the town, not the ranch, not—But that's old news," he finished, shutting her out.

Old news? Maybe it was, but not forgotten. Not by Brand, anyway, Faline realized. It must've had an enormous impact on him as a child, having a mother who was so unhappy. Then not having one at all.

Children, she knew, sometimes blamed themselves for such things, often felt that they were responsible for any problems the adults were dealing with. Had a six-year-old Brand somehow imagined that he was the one who'd created the rift between his parents? That he was the one who'd caused his mom to leave?

Faline was still speculating on the possibility when it dawned on her suddenly that Mrs. T. was gone, and she was completely alone with Brand.

She swallowed hard, vividly remembering that he was no longer a boy, but a full-grown, one hundred percent, warm-blooded male. And there wasn't another living soul for miles around, except the animals of course.

Alone with the Wildman. Drinking wine, sharing conversation. The setting was normal enough, but underneath ran a current of excitement. A tingle of anticipation mixed with the wine in her veins, working like an aphrodisiac in her blood.

The man across from her was as unpredictable as her own feelings. And the thin veneer of society offered no protection at all from his independent nature. He might twirl the glass stem gracefully in his hands one moment, but he could just as easily crush the crystal goblet into a thousand pieces. He might banter lightly with her, but if he wanted something else, something that went beyond the casual, there was nothing to stop him from taking it.

Nothing except her own instincts, which warned her to play it safe. And hope that he'd do the same.

She stood up, and let her napkin drop to the chair. "I'd better turn in." She gave an exaggerated yawn, smiling apologetically. "Must be the country air."

He pushed the wineglass away and rose, his piercing eyes burning into hers. "Of course, the country air."

She nodded politely. "I'm sure it's nothing that a night in bed won't cure."

He arched one eyebrow.

Faline looked down at the polished floorboards, her cheeks burning, her tortured mind wishing that Fang were here to swallow her up whole and out of sight. "You see, I'm *very* tired," she murmured.

"Yes, I do see, Wildcat. You'd better hightail it out of here. Quick."

Faline didn't wait to be told twice. She made her way to the bedroom at lightning speed, locking the door behind her.

True to Mrs. Twitchford's prediction, the lions were restless again that night, and Faline lay awake for hours, listening to the low, sultry sounds. She should have been kneeling by the bed, thanking merciful heavens that nothing had happened between them. But relief wasn't exactly the predominant emotion she felt. It was—heaven help her—curiosity.

She couldn't help wondering what *might* have happened if the evening had taken a different course. Or if Brand hadn't drawn back that last second in the darkroom.

She'd *wanted* him to kiss her. She knew that he'd wanted it, too, but for some reason, he hadn't acted on those feelings. Yet.

And that was what scared her the most. His compassion. His self-restraint. The merciful side of him that seemed to understand her far too well.

It wasn't just that he hadn't ravished her wildly, the way any self-respecting savage would have, but that some part of her had actually hoped he would.

Faline Eastbrook, the dutiful daughter, the career-minded woman, interested in some tiger trainer with a ponytail? His idea of culture was probably watching reruns of the *Wild Kingdom.* What did he have to offer a woman of the nineties besides a drop-dead smile and six feet of miraculous muscular *maleness*?

A heart, she thought grudgingly. Clearly the guy had heart. Why else would he convert a profitable cattle farm into a costly haven for injured animals?

And a sense of humor. Hadn't she read somewhere that a well-developed sense of humor was a sign of intelligence? Or was she simply trying to justify her feelings by endowing Weston with qualities he didn't really possess? Was she looking for an excuse to take a walk on the wild side?

No doubt about it, Brand was as wild as they came. He wasn't the man she'd been searching for all her life. He was the man she'd been *afraid* to find. The man who could make her cross that fine line from dreaming into doing. But he could also be her undoing.

The street-smart, cynical part of her was grounded in reality. The reality of a world where men like Scott were lurking, where geeks and cads and creeps waited around every corner. But Brand Weston was the stuff of which fantasies are made.

And the uncynical part of Faline was doing plenty of fantasizing.

But she hadn't come to this ranch to play Jane, no matter how enticing Tarzan was. She had a photo assignment to complete, a career to salvage, and a future waiting for her back in New York if the job turned out well.

She had a life, after all, a life that still existed many miles from here. She had responsibilities.

They were a heavy load to carry around sometimes, and tonight they felt like a cloak of lead that had settled around her shoulders. She'd trusted Scott with too many of her responsibilities before. She wasn't ready to hand them over to the first man who came along, even if he was altogether incredible, the most fearless, completely fascinating man she'd ever met.

Still, if only for a short time, she wanted to shed that heavy cloak of reality, and follow the Wildman through his jungle. She wanted to be with him, in ways she was just beginning to imagine. She wanted it like crazy.

Two doors away, Brand heard the lions growling as well, but he wasn't paying too much attention. His mind had more interesting problems to consider. Like the far-too-tempting photographer who was sleeping under his roof.

Two thin doors. Not much to stop him if he decided to change his mind, and show her how good it could be between them. But something was still holding him back. Concern for her welfare? Or for his own?

He'd bet it would scare the hell out of her, to see just how primitive he could be. A solitary beast tamer in the throes of an unfulfilled passion. It sure scared the hell out of *him.*

The physical part, that would be pure pleasure. For *both* of them. He knew how to make certain of that. It was the part that came after he wasn't sure how to handle.

No way was he going to put himself through that again. No way was he going to let her whet his appetite, then hit the road while he was still hungry for more. No way would he be able to keep his hands off her for two weeks.

"Take it easy, now. Fang isn't even out of his cage, yet." Brand's eyes were lit by the late-afternoon sun, his expression one of unholy amusement.

Take it easy? Faline repeated silently. She'd like nothing better. But somehow her body wouldn't listen to what her mind was telling it. The sight of the great tiger made her go rigid again. Even though the creature was behind bars at the moment, she knew that sooner or later he *wouldn't* be.

She glanced longingly at the forest path leading back toward the house. "Maybe I'd better go get my telephoto lens. The super high-powered one."

He shook his head. "Get a grip, Faline. I won't let you get hurt. I kind of like you in one piece."

A chivalrous savage. How charming. She glared back at him. "And how does Fang like me? Raw, no doubt."

He scanned the length of her body in open appreciation, working his way up from the sand-flecked tips of her tennis shoes, past the smooth bare legs clad in denim shorts, to the three-button opening of her sheer summer blouse. "An interesting thought. But it's unlikely that Fang will even touch you."

"Unlikely? I'd feel a lot better if you said it was definite." She turned toward the house. "Now, about that telephoto lens . . ."

She was jerked up short by a hand holding the back of her shorts. "Whoa there, Wildcat. It's too late to turn tail and run. I thought you were tougher than that."

She spun around in frustration, her arms crossed in front of her. "I *am* tough. But I never said anything about crazy."

He let her go suddenly, catching her off balance, sending her arms and legs sprawling skyward. Faline tried to regain her hold on gravity, grabbing at air, but the result was less than graceful, as she landed on the sandy forest floor.

"*Ouch!*" She glared up at him, trying to wipe the sand off her legs, struggling to maintain her composure. "I can't believe you did that."

Brand reached one well-muscled arm toward

her, offering a hand up. "Give me a break, woman. I didn't toss you on purpose."

Faline gave him a skeptical look. So maybe he hadn't done it on purpose. But did he have to stand there and look so sure of himself, so at ease and magnificent while she was coughing up sand? Did he have to use that word again? *Woman.* At a moment like this, it was just a little too much.

She took his hand, but all pretense of professionalism had left her. She was scared, angry, and frustrated with the whole situation. Frustrated with *him.* She saw an opportunity for some sweet revenge. She took it.

Instead of pulling herself up, she tightened her grip on his hand and jerked down, hard. If the sand hadn't been so soft and slippery, if the soles of his brown leather boots hadn't been quite so slick, her outrageous action might not have been so successful. But the laws of physics worked in Faline's favor, and brought the Wildman sliding down on top of her with a thud.

"*Umph.*"

The cloud of sand wafting around them blocked his face for a second or two, but when the dust finally cleared, his chest was flat against hers, his jean-clad legs locked over her bare ones, and he didn't look too pleased. At first. Maybe the laws weren't working in her favor after all.

He looked down at her, his eyes dark with desire. "I thought city girls were supposed to be polite. If this is really what you wanted, you should've asked. Nicely."

Faline felt her stomach knot with anticipation, uncomfortably aware of his hot, sandy body pressed suggestively against hers. Every hard inch of it. Her heart was fluttering from sheer expectation, but she wasn't about to let it show. She couldn't. She went on the defensive, instead.

"Then I'll ask you to take your paws off me. *Please.*"

He tightened his grip on her arms, pinning them over her head before she had a chance to think about struggling. "Not so fast." His breath was warm against her ear, tickling provocatively at the edge of her throat. "I think I'd like an apology first."

She stared at him incredulously. "You want *me* to apologize?"

His gaze raked over her body, settling again on her flushed face. "Unless you'd like to show me some other way?"

Faline nearly trembled when she imagined what he must be thinking. She knew exactly how she'd like to show him. A swift kick in the gut. A sharp knee somewhere more sensitive. Unfortunately, her knees were hopelessly trapped under the impressive weight of him.

"Anytime you're ready," he told her. "I don't mind waiting."

He studied her for another long, lazy minute, his eyes lingering at her thighs, her breasts, smiling in sympathetic understanding as her breathing became quick and erratic. If Faline had been standing, she would have buckled beneath that rough, seductive stare.

No man had ever looked at her that way before. It was outrageous, deliberate, *indecent.* And it was exciting her more than she dared to admit. He had to let go of her *now.* Before her trembling body gave her away.

"Fine," she muttered, glaring up at him. "I'm sorry. Are you satisfied now?"

He slackened the grip on her arms as his eyebrows rose in a mocking smile. "Satisfied? Lady, you must be joking. I've never been so far from satisfaction in my life."

"Oh," Faline mumbled, at a loss for words. She wasn't sure what to make of Weston's admitted arousal. But then, she hadn't had much experience with the complex mysteries of the male anatomy.

Scott's amorous ability was the only frame of reference she had, and he'd never displayed this kind of powerful virility in all the months she'd known him. The Wildman was a specimen unto himself, a prime, healthy male unlike any she'd ever met. Potent. Vigorous.

Maybe it had something to do with all this fresh country air. It was certainly having an effect on her.

She struggled beneath him, trying to get free, but stopped cold when Fang let out a low growl. A watch-tiger, she mused in irritation. Why couldn't the guy just have a dog?

"Fang doesn't like it when you're angry. Better make up with me quick, Wildcat, or you'll have another beast to answer to."

She scowled at the caged tiger, then made a face at Brand, but she couldn't help responding to the compelling laughter in his eyes. "I guess I am outnumbered," she admitted. "And I would like to get on with the work. Let me up, and I'm willing to call a truce."

Obligingly, he rolled over, and Faline stood to brush the sand off her arms and legs. Brand stayed there on the sandy ground, his chin propped carelessly in one hand, his head cocked casually to one side as he watched her with interest.

"Aren't you going to get up?"

He yawned and tossed back his ponytail. "Any minute now. Don't you have to load some film or something? Maybe change a lens? Take your time. I don't mind watching."

Faline shrugged and walked toward her trusty camera bag. She pulled the fifty-millimeter lens from its protective pocket and snapped it over the camera's shutter opening, letting out a quick sigh. It was now or never. "Well?" she said expectantly.

Brand rose to his feet in one easy movement and walked calmly to the tiger's cage. Fang padded menacingly toward the wire door, waiting to come out. Faline held her breath.

FIVE

Calling out a clear command, Brand released the latch on the tiger's cage. Fang bounded forward to greet his master.

"Whoa Fang, easy boy."

Faline took a step back, clutching the edge of her camera with hands that had gone suddenly moist. The tiger wasn't paying much attention to her at the moment, but at any second he could turn, and come toward her. There was nothing to stop him. No harness, no collar, no nice, safe leash. The only thing that stood between Faline and certain danger was the skill and bravery of a man she barely knew. A man who many believed to be off his rocker.

Faline swallowed hard, her heart beating a hundred miles an hour. Maybe she was the one off her rocker. Maybe she was taking the career thing a little too seriously. Was any assignment worth this kind of risk?

Brand whistled low and clapped his hands once. Fang responded by trotting in a slow circle around his trainer, then dropped to the ground with a muffled thud, waiting expectantly for the next command. Faline exhaled slowly, taking another few steps back. The tiger glanced her way, blinking in curiosity with intense green-gold eyes.

"Easy," Brand said in a cool voice. "Don't walk too quickly. He might mistake you for his prey."

Faline stopped dead in her tracks and whispered through gritted teeth. "*Now* you tell me."

Brand's teeth flashed white in the evening light. "It's okay to move. Just do it slowly. Remember to relax."

Faline rolled her eyes skyward. Who was he kidding? It was hard to relax when she could barely remember to breathe.

Fang rolled lazily onto his side and started cleaning one forepaw with a giant sandpaper tongue.

"See?" Brand said, gesturing to the contented tiger. "Fang's relaxed."

Faline sighed. It was easy to relax if your teeth were as sharp as steak knives and your body was built from four hundred pounds of functional feline muscle. It was a little harder to stay calm if you weighed less than a third of that size and your insides were several times softer.

Brand knelt, scratching Fang behind the ears,

nuzzling his face against the animal's glossy neck. Fang might've been an overgrown kitten the way the Wildman was handling him. Faline shook her head in awe. A heartwarming sight. A Kodak moment.

Cautiously, she raised the camera's viewfinder to eye level and pressed the shutter release. Fang lifted up on his haunches, a guttural, threatening growl emanating from behind bared ivory incisors. Faline's heart nearly stopped.

"Easy, Fang." Brand cuffed the tiger playfully on the ear, skillfully distracting him. "The lady prefers good manners."

"The lady prefers house cats!" Faline retorted under her breath.

As if he'd understood her perfectly, Fang swung his head around and growled again.

Brand quirked his mouth at the corners. "Better tell him you didn't mean it."

Faline gulped. "I take it back. I swear I take it back."

Fang settled down again, resting his head on one paw. Faline lowered her camera a little, eyeing the big cat carefully. Her hands were shaking. She'd have to settle down herself to take any decent pictures. The magazine editors were funny that way. They preferred their photos to be in focus.

"Try it again," Brand suggested. "Your shutter startled him the first time. He needs to get used to the noise."

Faline nodded, raised the camera back into position, and closed her eyes. *Click*.

Nothing happened. She opened her eyes wide again and looked around. Fang didn't growl this time, only blinked at her. Faline smiled, and some of the trembling subsided. Progress.

"Good," Brand commented, "but I'm sure the magazine wants more action. Try to move in closer, and I'll put Fang through his paces."

Faline took another deep, calming breath and watched in fascination as man and animal stood, performing a series of complex exercises. The communication between them was strong, two minds linked with a strange verbal and visual language that both understood. Some of the signals were incomprehensible to Faline, but the tiger was in tune to his master, and could stop, start, or walk in any direction according to the signs and sounds he was given.

Brand's low voice was full of praise and affection, and it was obvious that the tiger thrived on the contact. Fang wanted to please his master. Faline continued to watch them, feeling more out of place than ever. She had never seen a bond so strong between two living creatures. It was a relationship of perfect trust.

The sort of relationship she had never had.

She wondered how it would feel just to let go like that and open up one hundred percent to another person. To be so connected that there wasn't any need for words.

She walked forward a few paces, compelled by the awesome, intimate sight. Fang didn't seem to notice, and Faline was emboldened by her success. She took another step toward them, framed the scene in the viewfinder, and snapped the release.

Fang whirled around, roaring at her in displeasure. He crouched down low, nostrils flaring as he caught her scent. He arched his back and his rear paws dug for purchase in the sandy dirt, preparing to charge if she dared to approach.

Faline did not dare. She shut her eyes tight, imagining the headlines in *Camera* magazine. *Stupid Photographer Becomes Snack in the Line of Duty.*

As for her long-suffering parents—Mr. and Mrs. Eastbrook would have to bury her with the epitaph, "She should've had a real job." Their disobedient daughter had made her final, fatal, foolish choice. And poor Vail. His ten percent commission was about to become tiger chow.

"*Down!*"

The voice was like an anchor in a sea of fear, the tone cool and commanding. Faline opened her eyes. Never had she been so grateful for a strong male presence. Her self-defense teacher might be shocked to hear her say it, but a brawny man was handy to have around. A *brave* brawny man.

How else could you describe a guy who'd throw himself in front of a tiger to protect you?

Still skittish from the confrontation, Fang reared up on his hind paws, pushing his forelegs against Brand's wide chest. Upright, the animal looked even larger than before, looming over the Wildman like a storybook monster with a huge furry head and fierce glowing eyes. Still standing, they struggled against each other, paws locked with arms as they swayed together in an exotic dance of danger.

Faline found the struggle almost painful to watch. Every muscle in Brand's body was straining from the incredible effort, his arms bulging with steel and sweat, his jaw set in undeniable determination. It was a scene from ten thousand years ago, when men had to rely on their own strength and power to survive. Brand's face was contorted with sheer gut strength, with a wild, wrenching look of some early conqueror. Faline found it impossible to look away.

Instinctively, she pointed her camera toward the action, and started burning film. The shutter clicked at lightning speed, but neither man nor beast paid any attention. Faline was so caught up in the struggle, it took her a dozen frames to realize that Brand's will was the dominant one. Breathing hard, with a fine mist of moisture on his face, he finally pushed Fang forward, backing the tiger away from Faline.

Seconds later, Fang dropped down on four paws, his striped tail twitching in excitement, slapping hard against the coarse denim covering Brand's legs.

"*Down.*"

Brand's voice sounded again, but it was softer

this time, almost seductive in its calm, coaxing quality.

Fang settled to the ground at the Wildman's feet, and waited for his master's next bidding.

Faline's entire body went limp with relief. She was shocked to discover she'd taken an entire roll of film, but the scene between man and tiger was so fierce and fascinating, she'd simply been caught up in the moment. Now that the immediate danger had passed, her body started shaking again, a delayed reaction to her own fear.

"Don't sweat it. Fang just got a little weird on us. He'll calm down."

Faline tried to force a smile.

Brand shot her a quick look of concern. "Sit tight while I put him back in the cage. I think you've both had enough for one afternoon."

Faline nodded gratefully. She'd heard of job stress before, but this was ridiculous.

Even when the tiger was safely lounging in his bunker again, her trembling continued, but her mind felt a lot easier. Until Brand approached and wrapped his rock-solid arms around her, pulling her close.

"Easy. Just let it go."

Faline stiffened at first. Facing the tiger had been tough enough, but she'd managed to maintain some semblance of control over her own body. But this—this warm six foot wall of solid, comforting man was enough to do her in. The cradle of his arms was secure, sensual, *scary*.

"It's okay. We'll take it slow. Nice and slow."

His voice was low and rusty, reassuring. Faline felt the fear flowing from her limbs, the adrenaline burning itself out to be replaced by another emotion she couldn't quite describe. She went all soft and achy inside, her thoughts turning sweet and steamy. Nice and slow with Brand. The possibilities were endless.

"That's it, little one. Relax." He buried his head in the nape of her neck, his lips teasing the sensitive area behind her ear.

Faline fairly melted into the satisfying solidity of his chest. Tiny jolts of pure electric excitement were stealing into her veins. She pressed closer to the source of sheer male energy, her breasts so tight against his T-shirt, she could feel his corded muscles rippling beneath. The sensation left her weak.

She could feel her defenses starting to melt. She could almost begin to let go. Almost.

But just when she was beginning to relax, Brand stiffened, and the pinpricks of pleasure stopped shooting down her neck.

"Perfume," he said suddenly, and looked down at her in comprehension, raking one hand through his sun-lightened hair. "No wonder."

"Hmmm?"

Faline wasn't quite sure what he was talking about. She wasn't sure that she even cared. The only thing that seemed important at the moment was the incredible, hard-packed proximity of the

Wildman's body next to her own. And the dreamy, delicious way it was making her feel.

"Your perfume," he repeated. "I should've told you not to wear any."

Faline felt the haze clearing from her brain. "Don't you like it?"

He nodded slowly. "Believe me, *I* like it. It's Fang who seems to have a problem with it."

Faline blinked in indignation. "I'll have you know that *Eau so Chic* is the trendiest scent on the market right now."

"Sorry. Tigers have an infallible sense of smell. And Fang's subscription to the fashion magazines ran out months ago. Care to tell him he's out of style?"

Faline glanced nervously toward the cage. "You really think it could be my perfume?"

Brand inclined his head, letting the long golden ponytail fall to one side. "I really do. That's powerful stuff you're wearing. Imagine what it must be like for a big cat who can smell food at fifty yards. You're exciting him like crazy—like a double order of chicken necks."

Faline gave a wry smile. "How flattering. But I suppose that must be pretty enticing to a frisky tiger like Fang."

Brand grinned, shrugging his broad shoulders. "He's an animal."

Faline sighed. "Guess I'd better go wash it off."

His eyes raked swiftly across the scant cover of

her lightweight outfit. "The clothes ought to come off too."

"Excuse me?"

"They're full of perfume. You can't put them back on after your swim."

"My what?"

He gripped her by the wrist before she had a chance to walk away. "A swim in the pool. Just what you need to wash the perfume away. And what I need to cool off."

Faline knew they could both do with some cooling off, but she doubted that an evening interlude in Brand's secluded backyard pool was the way to do it. A cold shower was more what she had in mind. A long, cold shower.

"Sorry, I didn't bring a suit with me."

He gave her a languid, lazy smile. "No problem. I never wear one either."

Faline swallowed hard, trying not to let the scandalized look show too plainly on her face. She'd seen a lot living in the world's most cosmopolitan city. She wasn't supposed to be so easily shocked. But she knew all too well what would happen if she removed her clothes in front of the Wildman.

She knew it instinctively, from the growing awareness in her own body, and the powerful male response she'd read in his. The attraction between them had been instant, but something more intimate had been building from their very first touch. Some physical contact was inevitable, almost unavoidable, but to enter a pool together—naked? The results could be explosive.

"Guess I'll have a bath instead." She touched the nape of her neck where he'd kissed it. "I want to make sure it all washes off. Could take some scrubbing."

He studied her for several seconds, letting his eyes brush over her in one slow, erotic sweep. He finally settled his gaze on her lips and smiled faintly.

Faline's knees threatened to give out from under her. The Wildman could read her emotions as easily as he read his animals. He knew exactly what she was thinking. And from the crazy, erotic thoughts that were tumbling through her head it was pretty clear that she was attracted to him. He *knew* he could have her. And still he did nothing about it.

Was he leaving the decision up to her, giving her the opportunity to choose?

He released her hand carelessly, shrugging his shoulders. "Suit yourself. But the invitation stands if you care to join me later."

Faline nodded and watched him walk away, the lean rugged hips and long muscular legs disappearing through shadow-dark trees, melting into the twilight. She gathered up her equipment, treading slowly back to the house.

She was drained, almost let down after the roller-coaster experience of the afternoon. She should have been pleased that Brand respected her wishes so stoically, and yet—she wasn't. She'd wanted him to lead her to the water's edge, and coax her in with that low, languorous voice. But at the same time, she knew he'd never do it.

She had to follow her own lead this time, go with her gut instincts. He'd given her a choice, shown her that the power was in her hands. But that kind of freedom could be a scary thing. How to decide the right path, pick the least dangerous direction? Maybe it was wrong to avoid the danger altogether. Maybe it was the sweet taste of recklessness that she really craved.

Or was it the pull of the man himself? The complex mystery of him, the combination of strength and understanding and sexuality she'd never known before?

She entered the house just as Mrs. T was leaving, and they waved good night to each other in the fading light. Faline mounted the stairs to her room, still deep in thought, and stowed her equipment safely under the bed. Shedding her shorts and blouse for a comfy, oversize T-shirt, she drew a light cotton bathrobe around her, and walked to the tub to start the water. But a sudden flash of feeling and fantasy made her stop.

She couldn't help imagining the Wildman without his clothes. *Naked*, in the pool behind the house. At this very minute.

She put a hand to her temple and tried to shake the picture away. The job was definitely getting to her. Photography made a person think in such visual terms, she couldn't help *seeing* Brand in her head—stripped, wet, and stunningly handsome. A living work of art. She'd give anything to see it in person.

She sank down onto the bed, pulling tightly on a handful of blanket as she tried to hold herself in check. So what was stopping her? A strong sense of caution? A healthy dose of fear? A past that made taking emotional risks completely terrifying?

But she was here to put the past behind her, wasn't she? Impulsively, she rose from the bed, calmly knotted the belt on her thin robe, and padded down to the first floor in bare feet.

Her eyes squinted in the near darkness, her ears pricking at the faint sound of splashing in the backyard. Back forest was more like it. The pool was open to the sky, but surrounded by a dense stand of moss-laden oaks. She could see the water glimmering through the trees, pink and silvery, catching the last painted glow from the setting sun.

Her heart quickened as she stole out the back door, slipping through the trees like a night elf, tiptoeing silently over the soft sand and bracken. The pool of water grew larger, more moonlit blue as she approached, flashing in the starlight. Faline darted behind a large oak, her pulse pounding in her ears as she peered around the gnarled brown trunk.

The entire patch of water was visible now, shimmering and swirling with tiny waves lapping against the perimeter of earth-dark tile. It was a breathtaking sight, a large liquid jewel, melting in the middle of the sultry forest floor. At the far end a splash sounded, the water foamed to silver, and Brand's body rose through the rippling surface.

He flung his head back and stood upright in the shallow end, a sensuous bronzed statue, dripping with blue satin water and black velvet shadows. Residual drops of moisture glistened against his streaming hair, like pale blue sapphires raining on a cloth of gold. The wet gems sparkled down his bare arms and back, running in rivulets across the curving muscles of his chest, disappearing into the glowing pool of stars that lapped about his bare hips.

Faline darted back behind the tree and raised a hand to her mouth to quiet her quick, frantic breathing. Something had drawn her to this spot—curiosity, desire? She wasn't sure. But now that she'd found the Wildman, it didn't feel decent to be watching him like this. He didn't even know that she was there. Lord, she *hoped* he didn't know, because how would she ever explain it?

She peeked around the edge of the trunk again, to make sure he hadn't spotted her, and her heart started beating double time. He'd shaken the droplets free from the drenched, moisture-dark strands of his hair and was starting to climb the tiled steps that sloped up and out of the water. He was leaving the pool, every moist masculine inch of him. And Faline couldn't tear her eyes away.

She knew she should be leaving, *now*, while she

still had the chance. She ought to turn and run back to that nice safe room on the second floor as fast as her bare feet would carry her. But the magnificent sight of Brand, wet and naked, kept her rooted to the spot.

He continued his ascent from the pool, still mercifully unaware of her presence. The upper half of him had been nerve-racking enough, but when the lower half of that prime, primitive body emerged, sleek and soaking, Faline had to hold on to the tree for support. Well built was a term woefully inadequate to describe him. Well endowed was more like it. *Extremely* well endowed.

Faline let out a low gasp. She'd seen naked men before. She'd even photographed several nude models in Photography 201. But nothing could have prepared her for the fascinating, fearsome sight of Brand Weston, an untamed barbarian in the buff.

Involuntarily Faline's eyes were focused on the damp, clinging patch of hair that thrust down between his legs, drawing her incredulous gaze to the most forbidden, almost frightening part of his anatomy. A sharp thrill ran through her at the intimidating sight.

She pressed a hand to her chest, wondering if her heart could stand the excitement much longer. She'd never seen a man so perfectly put together. Her street smarts deserted her. Instead of a clever observation, the only expression that came to mind was *Oh my.*

She tried to detach herself emotionally, and simply study Brand Weston as if he were another subject to be captured by her camera. But even in her professional opinion, she couldn't find a single weak angle. The man didn't have a "bad side." He was flawlessly and shockingly sexy, from the top of his high, chiseled cheekbones, all the way down to his . . . ankles.

Faline sank against the tree, weak from the sheer sight of him. What to do now? She couldn't stay any longer and run the unthinkable risk of discovery. She had to get away before he spotted her and made her pay for her impertinence.

She wasn't exactly ashamed of her brash behavior, rather she was more than a little amazed. She had never, ever done anything so daring before. A few days ago, she wouldn't have even dreamed of it.

But being isolated on this secluded ranch with a man like Weston had changed her somehow. She was learning that life's possibilities were endless. She was learning that prudence and common sense couldn't always keep you from harm. And that too much caution could shut out the most beautiful fantasies.

And tonight the fantasy had turned to reality.

Tonight she'd stood staring in the moonlight, at a man who wasn't hers, and brazenly watched him bare everything. She'd let him believe that he was alone. She'd studied him wantonly when she might have looked away. And what was worse, she'd enjoyed it.

She *deserved* to be caught in the act. She had a sudden urge to go to him and confess what she'd done, but somehow she didn't dare. She wasn't crazy enough to expect mercy from a damp, naked beastmaster. Especially when he had every right to be angry.

A rustling noise from Brand's direction drew her attention, and she held her breath as he slung a towel low around his hips, and knotted the ends just below his waist. Faline closed her eyes and pressed her body closer to the tree trunk, trying her best to blend into the shadows.

The wise thing to do was to wait it out, let him walk back to the house alone, oblivious to her presence. Then she'd slip inside and up to her bedroom at the first opportunity. He'd never have to know that she'd been there.

A simple plan.

A major miscalculation.

Tigers weren't the only creatures with heightened senses, or so Faline realized when she heard the low, lazy voice behind her. Brand's ears must've been perfectly in tune to the night around them, perceptive enough to pick up on her single, soft gasp. Unfortunately, the realization came too late.

"Enjoying the view?" His tone was warm but the words were mocking.

Faline bit her lower lip and buried her face

against the rough tree bark. She wouldn't, *couldn't* turn around to face him. And even if she could, what was there to say?

"Look at me."

She cringed, and her whole body resisted the command. She *had* looked at him. Like she'd never looked at anyone else in her life. That was the problem.

"You didn't mind it a few minutes ago," he chided softly.

Faline spun around, her mortification forgotten for a moment. "You knew I was here the whole time."

His eyes glittered, bright with starlight. "Yes."

She folded her arms across her chest, protecting herself from that penetrating stare. "You might've said something."

It was a weak argument, and she knew it, but he didn't press his advantage. He simply arched his eyebrows at her and propped an arm against a low tree branch, leaning over her. The movement dragged his towel loincloth down an inch or so, and it took a tremendous amount of willpower for Faline not to lower her gaze. Another stretch like that, and the terry-cloth covering could drop at any moment. A fascinating thought, since she'd already had an eyeful of what was underneath.

"The light's a little low for taking pictures," he observed. "So what *are* you doing out here, woman?"

She swallowed nervously, willing to let the last

word pass this time. "Guess I changed my mind about that swim. But I can see you're already finished. Maybe some other time."

She turned to head for the house, the warm golden light from the upstairs bedroom beckoning her to safety.

"Not so fast," he purred, tugging at the belt on her robe and pulling her back toward him.

Faline stared up at him, breathless, mesmerized by the hot, hypnotic look in his eyes. She didn't move as he expertly unknotted her cotton belt and snaked it out of the confining loops and away from her waist. The edges of her robe draped open, revealing the loose T-shirt and a long stretch of bare legs.

Brand stepped back, smiling with undisguised interest. "Go ahead and take your swim, Faline. The water's just right. And this time it's my turn to watch."

SIX

"Your turn?" she squeaked, backing away from the tree and toward the pool. "I didn't mean to watch you like that. Actually, I was just . . ."

"Just coming out to swim, right? So now's your chance. Are you going to take that robe off and get in, or do you need some help?"

Faline could well imagine the kind of "help" he had in mind. She took a few more tentative steps to the pool, keeping a wary eye on Brand. Swim or him. Not much of a choice.

She glanced down at the cool shining water, deliciously dark except for a pale shaft of moonlight and a handful of stars reflected across its glassy surface. It *did* look inviting. If she'd been alone she wouldn't have hesitated for a second. But she had an interested audience of one, and he expected a private performance.

Her robe still draped comfortingly around her,

Faline dipped one foot into the shallow end, testing the temperature. It was warm and silky to the touch, beckoning her to slip in. She glanced back at Brand, and he folded his arms across his chest, waiting.

It struck her suddenly that she liked having him look at her that way. She liked the sharp thrill that ran through her as his mouth curled expectantly. She liked the idea of letting loose, and letting him watch her do it. Wasn't that what he'd been trying to show her all along? That it was possible to give of herself without losing herself completely?

For once, Faline Eastbrook had a chance to do something that wasn't so safe. She *wanted* to give him a performance. And she wanted it to be one he'd never forget.

She lifted her chin, her eyes still focused on the Wildman as she let the robe drop slowly past her shoulders and slip silently to form a soft cotton puddle at her feet. Brand didn't move, but he didn't take his eyes off her either.

Faline felt her senses heighten to a fever pitch. Every inch of her trembling skin was alight with sparks from the Wildman's eyes. She bit her lower lip, afraid her body wouldn't please him, *afraid it would.*

Descending several steps into the pool, she let the water lap around her thighs until it touched the hem of her T-shirt. The moist material clung tightly to the top of her legs, weighing the rest of the fabric down until it pulled smooth and taut, rubbing gently against her unbound breasts.

"Keep going." His voice was hoarse.

Faline smiled inwardly. She knew she was getting to him. But this whole fantasy scene was starting to get to *her*. Her body was so warm, she half expected to see steam rising from the water as she entered. And the way Weston was watching her! How much could one woman take?

She dropped the neckline of her shirt down low over one shoulder, preparing to pull it off, but after a moment's hesitation, realized that she *couldn't*. If Brand wanted to watch her swim, he'd have to take her just the way she was, T-shirt and all. With one fast, final movement, she plunged in the rest of the way, diving headfirst into the murky darkness.

Watching her from the side, Brand scanned the surface of the pool, wondering where the nymph would come up for air. He could use some extra oxygen himself, especially after that pseudo-striptease she'd put him through. For a moment he'd imagined she would actually go through with it, that she'd finally decided to give in, the way he'd wanted her to. The way he knew she could, given the right kind of help.

But at the last minute she'd seemed to lose her nerve. At the last minute her defenses had gone up again.

When he'd first found her by the tree, with those green eyes melting at him, warm with embarrassment and unspoken desire, he'd guessed that she was ready to trust in him. Ready to give what he knew was his for the taking. But the second she'd disappeared underwater, he knew he'd guessed wrong.

The big-town lady was still a little uptight. Those enormous green eyes were telling him one thing: *Touch me*, they pleaded. *Make love to me now, take me to paradise.* But the rest of her was still trying to keep a safe distance.

An amusing thought, since there was no such thing as safety from a determined wildman. He'd been content to let her keep that false sense of security for the time being, until she finally realized for herself that she didn't need it. Not with him.

The danger didn't lie in their coming together. It lay in the inevitable good-byes. He'd finally decided it might be worth it in the end. He'd decided to wait until she was ready. But there was nothing to stop him from coaxing her along.

Her body broke the water at the deep end, her wet T-shirt swirling around her like a ghostly cloud, soaking up moonlight. "See?" she asked, shaking the liquid from her streaming velvet hair, "No more perfume. Mission accomplished."

Her mission, perhaps. Definitely not his.

He blinked at her, his eyelids heavy. "I'm sure Fang will appreciate it."

Lord knows, he did. He liked the way the soaking fabric clung to her shoulders, molding itself around the slippery mounds of her pale breasts and the darker nipples beneath. He liked the way her skin glistened, wet and slick. Waiting for his touch.

She paddled there awhile, dipping and turning in the water, like a night siren calling to him in some ancient, unspoken language. He was tempted to join her, to answer the song, but her eyes still held a hint of hesitation. She rolled onto her back, her feet tickling the surface with small purposeful kicks, the peaks of her chest bobbing in and out of the dark wavelets, bright and dripping.

He strolled to the edge of the pool, watching all the while, enjoying her pleasure. From the corner of his eye, he saw the cotton puddle of her robe and walked over to pick it up.

"What are you doing?" Her voice was wary.

He hooked a finger inside the empty collar and held it up, considering. "Just waiting. I'll hang on to this until you're ready."

"Put it back! I can't get out like"—she glanced down at her tissue-sheer top, an intriguing look of confusion on her face—"like *this.*"

He waved the robe gently in the air on the end of an index finger. "Guess your other option is to stay in the water. Sure hope you like swimming—a *lot.*"

She scowled at him. Brand was definitely beginning to enjoy himself. He strolled slowly back to the large oak and hoisted himself onto a low branch, hanging the robe on a nearby limb like some sensual, suggestive trophy. "Come and get it," he whispered.

Faline glared at him, secretly wishing the branch would give way and send every intimidating inch of muscle-packed flesh to the sandy floor. It would take nothing less to wipe that cocky, self-assured smile from his much-too-handsome face. If ever a man realized that he held all the cards, this one did. And not even fate would step in to save her from him tonight.

"Turn around, then," she said hopefully.

Brand's teeth shone white in the moonlight. "No thanks. I'd rather enjoy the view."

Her heart was beating faster now, as she realized what was coming. She'd be finishing that show for him after all. But instead of a striptease it had turned into a wet T-shirt contest. And the audience was ready and waiting. "Is this how you treat all your female houseguests?" she asked in desperation.

His long, sun-darkened legs swung patiently back and forth against the lower branches. "Only the ones who sneak around to spy on me at night. I'm shocked by your lack of civilized manners, Ms. Eastbrook."

Faline's face flushed hot with anger and embarrassment. Did he have to remind her? "An eye for an eye, is that what you have in mind? Another savage law of the jungle, no doubt."

He rubbed his chin thoughtfully, a searing grin on the strong, shadowed face. "More like an eyeful for an eyeful."

She sent a shower of pool water splashing in his

direction, but missed her mark by several feet. "Very amusing. But the joke's over now. Hand me the robe."

The golden eyes blinked at her with interest. "Who's joking?"

"But I need something to cover up with," she insisted, her arms shivering from the cooling night air, or from the determined look in his eye. She wasn't sure which.

Brand dropped one hand to his waist, to the single, entirely unreliable knot that held the makeshift loincloth snug across his hips. "Maybe you'd like my towel instead. It's nice and warm. Plenty of body heat."

"Dddddon't take it off!" She held up a hand in protest. She couldn't go through *that* again. But her teeth were starting to chatter now and she had to do something. The thought of body heat, or any heat for that matter, was a compelling one. She took a few watery steps toward the shallow end.

Brand didn't take his eyes off her. He just kept staring in the most heathenish way. Like some bronzed pagan, waiting for the sacrifice to begin.

"Talk about manners," she muttered under her breath, mounting the first step out of the water.

"Barbarians are usually better off without them," he laughed, but the look on his face was anything but humorous. It was brutish, untamed, and blatantly sexual.

When the night air hit the rest of her body, Faline let out a sudden gasp. The rush of cold was a stunning shock to her system, pricking every pore and nerve ending with an icy jolt of stimulation. Yet another feeling ran beneath the cold, a hot, electric sensation, that made her feel raw, as though her skin had been singed by fire.

Brand leapt down from his branch. "What is it, Wildcat?"

She couldn't quite meet his eyes. For a modest woman, who'd never shown herself to a man this way, the experience was almost too intense to bear. Too frightening, too painfully sharp, too exciting.

"I can't," she whispered. "You don't understand."

"Try me."

She looked away, still afraid to face him. "Remember what I told you about my ex-partner? About being betrayed? Well, it's hard to forget the hurt. I just don't think I'm capable of this. I'm not capable of opening up again."

Not in the way he wanted her to. Not in *every* way. Not only was her body completely exposed, almost naked before him, but her emotions were on the line as well. She was on view, vulnerable. In some ways it was *worse* than being naked.

The T-shirt was splayed across every inch of her soaking skin, revealing the curves and peaks of her body in high, creamy contrast. Her nipples were erect from the cold—dark budding tips that stretched the sheer gauzelike fabric, tingling as they grew taut and hard against it.

She was aroused, and he hadn't even touched

her yet. She hated for him to see it, to see her like this. It was a wordless admission of her own desire. One look, and he would know just how badly she needed him.

"You are capable, Faline," he reassured her. "You're already halfway there."

Half frozen was more like it, she decided. From the cold. From fear. "Brand—" The word escaped before she had a chance to bite it back. She was asking for his help, but the idea didn't seem so terrifying anymore. Just this once, she could allow herself the luxury of it. She didn't have to be strong all the time.

He pulled the robe from the tree branch and came quickly forward, covering her with it. "Your body's like ice. Come here."

Faline let herself be drawn to him, gravitating toward his warmth like a night moth flying dangerously close to a burning bulb. He picked her up and carried her to the base of the oak tree, sheltering her against it, his body overlapping hers. His hands massaged gently across her back, her arms, her legs, rubbing heat into her with long, rhythmic strokes.

"Better?"

She was still shivering slightly, but it definitely wasn't from the cold. "Mmm-hmm."

"I'll take that as a yes," he said, but his hands didn't stop their skilled manipulation. They were working their way down her neck, kneading the tense muscles at her nape, willing every inch of her to relax against him.

"Yes," she sighed.

Brand's caress grew softer, his fingers stroking repeatedly against the downy surface of her skin. "Tell me when you want me to stop."

Faline nodded, only half coherent. She never wanted him to stop. She wanted it to go on and on, until every muscle had melted languidly away. She buried her head against his chest, drinking in the clean, cool smell of him, nuzzling her face softly against his skin.

Brand groaned and lifted her to her feet so she stood facing him, her back to the oak tree.

Faline looked up in dreamy confusion. "But I didn't ask you to stop."

"Open your robe for me, Wildcat."

With trembling hands, she pulled the edges back until the length of her body was bathed in moonlight.

Brand's eyes kindled at the sight, and his voice grew rough. "Better tell me to stop now, Faline. Play it safe."

She felt a thrill of alarm at the words, but her response to them was even more shocking. She took his hand in hers and guided it gently to cup one aching breast.

A low moan escaped him, and he pushed her up against the tree, taking her mouth to his. His breath was coming quick and warm on her lips as he parted them with his tongue, probing slowly inside her. Faline whimpered at the light butterfly strokes, almost losing control as he deepened the kiss, seducing her with the sweet, hot taste of his passion.

From that point the Wildman got very wild, very fast. His hands were on her buttocks, lifting her off the ground, pressing her back to the tree for balance as her legs straddled his waist. "Stay with me, Faline. Come with me tonight."

Faline's arms went around his head, drawing him closer as she let out a startled, shaking sigh. He buried his face in the base of her throat, raining bird-wing kisses down to the lush softness of her breasts. Violent shock waves of feeling rocked through her, sending sharp spears of pleasure racing to every delicate nerve ending.

Brand let out a low growl, hiking the edge of her T-shirt up over her legs, exposing her bare midriff and damp panties to his bold, insistent caress. "Let it go, baby. Just relax and let me take you there."

Faline was still astride him, drowning in the dizzy feel of sex-stiffened muscle, sleek golden hair, and warm slippery skin. His touch strengthened in intensity, turning urgent, primal, and she let out an involuntary shudder, half in anticipation, half in fear of his growing need of her. A need that was primitive, raw, abandoned. *Terrifying.*

Brand swore softly as he felt her body grow tense against him. The chemistry between them was still too new, too frightening for Faline just to let go and put her faith in him. She was still afraid to trust fully. Until that happened, if it ever happened, she would never be his. Not even for one night. Not in the way he wanted her to be. Finally, completely, unreservedly.

He tore his mouth away, jerking his head back to stare into her eyes. Eyes that were pleading for mercy, begging him for more, and at the same time, afraid he might not stop. Brand wasn't sure he could stop. She was so warm, so responsive, reacting irresistibly to his touch, moving against him with a slow rocking sweetness that could drive a man crazy.

Did she know how close to the edge she'd driven him? Judging by the look of innocent fear in those emerald depths, she probably had a pretty good idea. But as barbaric as he might be, aroused even to the point of pain, he was still a thinking, rational man, and he knew it was wrong to take her this way. He couldn't claim her body until her spirit was fully engaged.

"You stopped," she said, breathless, relieved, disappointed.

He set her back on her feet, groaning in silent agony. He was disgusted with his own nobility. Any self-respecting savage would've ravished first, asked questions later. "You wanted me to."

Her face flushed beautifully against the creamy skin. "I—I'm not sure."

His hand cradled the soft curve of her cheek,

gently stroking. "Neither am I. I didn't plan it this way."

He'd planned to follow through, to make indulgent, unconditional love to her, to make her helpless with pleasure, crazy with need until she begged him to be set free. So what the hell was wrong with him?

Regretfully, he watched her drag the T-shirt back down over her belly and close the robe protectively against his interested gaze. It helped him a little. At least he wouldn't be visually reminded of what he'd given up.

But the picture of her wet, half-naked body would be etched forever in his brain. Slow, burning torture. A just punishment for a softhearted savage. Exactly what he deserved for being so honorable.

She bent to retrieve the cotton belt from the ground. "I don't understand."

Her voice was still soft and shaky, still aroused. Brand felt the tight catch of desire deep in his groin. God, but he was a fool. He might've had her, here, now. In every way he could imagine. Every way but one.

His jaw muscles tightened. "It's simple. This isn't some game we're playing. This is serious. The real thing. And I don't think you're ready to handle it."

She bit her lower lip and stared up at him, her eyes enormous. "I can take care of myself."

He laughed softly and let his gaze slide back

over her in blatant contradiction of her words. "You'll have to prove that to me later, Faline. Much later."

Faline didn't sleep well that night; her dreams were filled with monsters even more menacing than the ones she'd faced during the day. Later, the midnight fantasies turned erotic, and she tossed back and forth in yearning frustration. She woke before dawn and tiptoed downstairs to the comfort of her darkroom.

Of course Brand was probably still asleep, completely unaware of the inner chaos he'd caused in her. She'd love to stroll sweetly into his bedroom and dump the whole vat of developer over his head. Come to think of it, she could think of better things to do to him in that bedroom. Come to think of it, she couldn't think of much else.

She loaded the film from the day before into the lightproof canister, sighing in confusion as the scenes from last night flashed uncensored through her mind. He'd scared her. She had to admit, she'd been a little afraid when Brand got so hot and bothered. He'd been almost out of control.

But what was she so afraid of? What would've happened if she'd really let go, the way he'd wanted her to? He wouldn't have hurt her. She knew that instinctively. And if instinct wasn't enough, he'd proved it to her by throwing himself in front of Fang. He'd *saved* her from a tiger. What more tangible evidence of trust could a woman want?

The worst thing that could've happened was a night of incredible, unadulterated physical pleasure. Followed by some serious emotional repercussions. And that was precisely what frightened her.

One night in the Wildman's arms wouldn't be enough. He'd asked for more than just her body, he'd asked her to give herself to him, to commune with him body and soul. He wasn't a simple savage, after all, but a complex adult male, who expected nothing less from her than complete unquestioning trust. A lot to ask of a woman who'd been betrayed before, whose middle name was wary.

She sighed again, running the film through the orderly maze of solutions, rinsing off the last chemical traces with water and inspecting the final results under the bright closet light. Her jaw dropped in astonishment. The pictures were some of the best she'd ever taken.

The action shots were downright amazing, with Brand and the tiger facing off, lean muscle against sleek animal fur. Two untamed males locked in mortal combat, frozen by her camera for the world to see. She hung the long reel of negatives on a rack to dry and darted back upstairs, her confidence bolstered by the positive results.

She'd make the prints as soon as possible and send them to Vail for a surprise preview. He'd be so pleased. She was finally starting to put Scott's betrayal behind her and get on with her work.

She paused momentarily at the entrance to her bedroom, listening for the sound of Brand's regular breathing only two doors down. Was he still asleep, she wondered, or feeling some of the same frustration she'd endured through the night? It was hard to imagine what sexual denial would do to a man as virile as Weston. The thought of it gave her renewed respect for his self-control.

Curious, she stole toward the open doorway of his room, and looked inside.

He was sitting up in bed, his sleep-tousled hair falling in sexy waves about his face, his body naked except for a white sheet bunched in a significant pile below his waist. He looked back at her, the drowsy gaze clearing from his eyes.

"Faline," he called softly. "Don't you know a man's bedroom is dangerous first thing in the morning? Or have you had a change of heart since last night?"

SEVEN

Faline gulped in uncomfortable surprise. She hadn't expected him to be awake. And as for his comment about bedroom dangers—she'd heard that men were friskier in the morning, but she'd never seen a living, breathing example of this mysterious phenomenon. Until now.

"But it's nearly breakfasttime!" she protested. A weak argument, she knew, but he'd caught her completely off guard.

His eyes glinted in amusement. "Exactly."

Faline backed cautiously away from the doorjamb. How could one man look so barbarous and so incredibly sexy all at the same time?

"How about some nice eggs and bacon?" she suggested sweetly.

His gaze raked appreciatively over her short nightgown and bare feet. "How about some breakfast in bed? Right now."

"I'm going down to eat." She turned away from him and headed back to her bedroom, aware that she was being watched from the rear. She hoped the nightgown wasn't as sheer as she remembered, and that the sight of her in it wouldn't make his morning hormones go into dangerous overload.

She had every right to worry, Brand thought as he watched her premature exit. He felt as if someone had kicked him hard in the groin. A result of last night's unfinished interlude, he realized. Another evening *almost* with her, and he'd wind up in intensive care.

"Save some for me," he called after her. He sure as hell wasn't going to track her down and drag her back bodily to his bed, no matter how good it was likely to be. If they ever did make love, she would come to him willingly, submitting freely to his desires and to her own. She would learn to drop her guard, to let down all those defenses and trust in him. And if it didn't happen that way, it wouldn't happen at all.

"Faline, sweetie, what's happening to you down there? Have you gone completely native, or caught a tropical disease of some sort?"

Vail's voice sounded as loud, clear, and sarcastic as if he'd been in the same room with her instead of at his office back in New York. Faline sighed. Although it'd been only a few days since she'd sent the photos, she'd expected a phone call any day. Except she'd been hoping for a few more compliments and a little less attitude.

"I'm fine," she lied. If fine came under the heading of anxious days spent around a nervous tiger and sleepless nights spent apart from his owner.

"Fine!" he scoffed. "Sweetcakes, your voice sounds about as high-strung as a Stradivarius. And these pictures"—there was a long, pregnant pause—"they're *un*-believable."

Faline smiled. "Pretty great, huh?"

Vail let out a sharp laugh. "Great? Honey, they're so hot, they're smokin'! Trouble is, I can't send them to *Eco*. They'd laugh me out of the business."

Faline clutched the receiver. "You can't—I thought you said they were *hot.*"

"Sizzlin', sweetie. But this isn't some *Cosmo* centerfold you're workin' on. It's a back-to-nature magazine. And I do mean nature. Trees, animals. No people. Tarzan's got to go."

"Tarzan?"

"The model. The guy with the tiger. I don't know where you found him, darlin', but it's easy to see how you got sidetracked. The body's incredible. But you'll have to ditch him anyway. Send him to New York. I can get him five figures a month."

Faline bit her lower lip, trying not to scream. She didn't want to argue with Vail, she just wanted to weep with frustration. "He's not a model, Vail.

That's the tiger trainer. Wildman Weston, the crazy recluse, remember?"

There was a long pause, followed by a sharp intake of air. "*That's* Weston? The owner of the ranch? Fal, sweetie, you're in bigger trouble than I thought."

She glared at the phone, indignant. "I don't know what you're talking about."

She could almost hear him smirking over the line. "You're losing your professional perspective—over some hunky hick in blue jeans. Sure, the guy's gorgeous—an aesthetic Adonis. But the editors want cat shots, not pinup posters. What do they put in the water down there, anyway? Vitamin E?"

She twisted the telephone cord slowly around her fingers, wishing it was one of Vail's overpriced neckties. At the moment, she would gladly have wrapped it around his throat, but it was hard to argue with someone when you knew he was right. She *had* lost her perspective.

Of course the dominant subject in the photos shouldn't be the Wildman. It just happened that he was the dominant subject in her mind. It also happened that Fang had stayed skittish around her and the camera all week, sensing the tension in the air, and he hadn't let her get within twenty feet.

She lifted her chin. "I get the message, Vail, don't worry."

He sighed heavily into her earpiece. "But I am worried, Fal. It's just not like you to lose your focus. Better get the job finished and get out of there before that aborigine wants to sacrifice you as a virgin or something."

Faline smiled ruefully. "Not much chance of that I'm afraid."

"Well, you're a virgin in spirit, sweetie, and that guy looks wild enough to do almost anything." He shuddered dramatically.

"He's not a maniac, Vail. He's barely even touched me." She grimaced slightly, guiltily aware that she hadn't told the entire truth.

The night by the pool had been the most exciting encounter she'd ever had with a man, but Brand had exhibited a superhuman amount of self-restraint. She almost wished that he had been more of a maniac that evening and persuaded her to make love despite her fears. At least it would have saved her from the past week of physical longing.

"So there shouldn't be a problem," Vail told her. "Just take the camera off Tarzan and focus it on the cats. Meow, meow. Get the picture?"

When Faline hung up, she realized it was time to face the situation head-on. She *had* to get some good shots of that tiger, and at this point she was willing to try just about anything. *Focus.* That's what she needed.

And the first step toward it was turning her major distraction into her major ally. Maybe Brand had some suggestions that might help. He was an animal behaviorist after all, with advanced training in biology. There were brains behind the body, and it was time to put them to good use.

She waited until breakfasttime the next morning, then asked him hopefully, "So what do you suggest?"

Brand took a long gulp of his coffee, eyeing Faline warily over the rim of his cup. Did she really mean it? Was she finally starting to come around and put just a little bit of faith in him? Was she finally beginning to open up? It was the opportunity he'd been waiting for all week. The first break in the barrier between them.

"I have a few ideas left," he said cautiously. "But you probably won't like 'em."

"Try me."

Wasn't that what he'd been attempting to do all along? "First you'll have to dump the camera," he said simply.

"Dump the—?"

"That's right. And don't look at me like that. I told you you weren't going to like it."

"But the camera—"

"Can wait. We need to work on you first."

"Oh. On me?"

He hesitated, afraid to put it too bluntly and destroy the progress they'd already made. But he knew Faline was strong enough to withstand the truth. And it was something she needed to hear. "I think you know what I'm talking about, Faline. The problem isn't Fang or the equipment or anything else. It's your fear."

She didn't protest at first, just gave him a thoughtful, "I see."

He'd hoped she would. For both their sakes. He wanted to help her. He wanted the photos to turn out well just as badly as she did.

Maybe even more. He wouldn't have his peace of mind or body back until Ms. Eastbrook had safely returned to New York. *Before* they got too deeply involved. Hell, it might already be too late for him. Even if she went back now, he doubted that he would ever be the same.

He polished off his coffee in two quick gulps and rose from the table, motioning for her to follow. "Well? What'll it be?"

She hesitated, one last time. "But I don't understand how—"

He snagged her by the shoulder and pulled her toward him, his eyes involuntarily lingering on her lithe body, on the sweet, shaky look that crossed her face.

"Faith, Wildcat. You gotta have it."

Faith? Faline wondered if he was asking the impossible. She'd traded that emotion in the day that Scott had walked out on her. And now Brand wanted her to put her faith in—what? A four-hundred-pound tiger as unpredictable as an overgrown alley cat? A hermit, who didn't have the slightest understanding of the word danger?

She stared up at him, hoping for some reassurance in that hard, handsome face. He didn't smile, or make mundane promises that everything would be okay, but the steady, unwavering gaze helped Faline to ground herself in reality. He was so sure of himself, so sure of *her* that words were not necessary between them. Brand could communicate without speaking, and the look he gave her was one of cool, silent confidence. *Come with me*, he said. *There's no reason to be afraid.*

Faline left her equipment behind and followed him out the door. They made the short trip through the forest in silence, approaching Fang's cage just as the morning sun broke through the trees. The big cat was stretched out on the ground, yawning hugely after a night of undisturbed rest, but he stood expectantly as they drew nearer. The great eyes blinked at Faline with glittering feline curiosity.

Brand stopped and turned toward her, his arms folded across his chest. "Another idea I had. The best one yet. Take off your shirt."

"My shirt?" She gave a nervous laugh, not quite sure if he was joking or not. Hoping that he was.

But Brand didn't laugh back, only kept watching her in that intense way.

"If that's your idea of faith—" she protested.

"It is."

She didn't budge. She *couldn't.*

"It's your choice," he told her softly. His voice was steady, rock-solid, reassuring.

She put a hand up to the collar of her blouse,

clutching tightly at the top button. "I don't suppose you'd be willing to offer an explanation."

He ran a hand across his lower jaw, thoughtful. "Would it help?"

She nodded.

"I was looking at your clothes this morning," he told her. "And it occurred to me that you ought to be wearing something else. My shirt, for instance. I think Fang would find you easier to accept."

She gave him an uncomprehending stare. "I don't get it. Why would he care? Is white his favorite color or something?" She glanced at Brand's button-down shirt, island cut, of lightweight cotton. A fashion-conscious tiger? She seriously doubted it. So what was Brand talking about?

"Remember the perfume?" he asked patiently, his eyes unreadable.

Faline felt a hot flush spreading across her body. Remember it? She'd been trying to put the episode out of her mind all week. "Sure," she said casually.

"Fang's senses are fine-tuned for scent. It's as strong as sight and sound for him. So if you're wearing my shirt, you'll have my smell on you. He's already learned to accept my scent, he's used to it. It should help him learn to accept you."

Faline nodded slowly, unable to argue with the implicit logic. It was an excellent idea, of course. "I suppose it's worth a try," she admitted softly.

"Uh-huh," Brand agreed calmly. "Faith, remember?"

She swallowed hard, reaching for the top button of her blouse. "You could at least turn around."

His eyes drifted to her face. "I could, but it's nothing I haven't seen before. Seen and enjoyed. A beautiful body is nothing to be ashamed of. Don't hide it from me."

Faline took a deep breath and started working on the buttons one by one. The process seemed to take forever, especially since Brand didn't take his eyes off her the whole time. It was the thought of him watching her that made her hands tremble. But there was another sensation deep in the pit of her stomach, a strange vibrancy that held the promise of the future, exciting and unknown.

She tugged at her shirttails, loosening them from the waistband of her shorts, and pulled them free, working cautiously on the last button. She hesitated, looked up, and met his eyes.

"Don't turn back now," he told her. "The first step's always the hardest."

She let her shirt drift open, revealing the soft satin of her bra and a semisheer wisp of lace that skimmed across the top of her breasts. She heard a quick intake of breath—Brand's? Her own? Her senses had heightened to the point where she couldn't tell, where both of their bodies seemed to be sensually in tune to each other, perfectly synchronized for mutual awareness.

"Wildcat, you are one brave, beautiful woman."

Faline drew strength from his words, reveling in his encouragement and admiration as she dropped the blouse below her shoulders, and finally removed it completely. She stood in front of him, her head held high, wearing nothing but her bra and shorts. Her outward composure might be fine, but inside she was still quivering like crazy.

After several tension-filled seconds, Brand seemed to recall himself and quickly stripped off his own shirt. He slipped it around her, buttoning the front with a gentleness she found surprising. Wearing Brand's shirt affected her as palpably as her own near nakedness.

The crisp cotton was still warm with his body heat, and gave off a faint musky scent that was purely masculine, raw and intoxicating. Even more compelling than the feel of his shirt against her skin was the sight of Brand *without* it. Breathtaking, beautiful. She glanced quickly toward Fang, trying to take her mind off the lean, corded muscles and smooth, sinewy skin.

"You okay?" Brand asked quietly.

Faline nodded. Surprisingly, she did feel okay. Better than okay. She felt free, unafraid, excited even. She hugged her arms to her chest and drew in a deep breath, drinking in the cool, comforting scent of the shirt and the clean smell of the forest at morning. Anything was possible.

"We could try him on the leash first," Brand

suggested skeptically. "But sooner or later it'll have to come off."

Faline shook her head. A big cat wearing a leash and collar wasn't what the *Eco* editors had in mind. And if she'd wanted pictures of caged animals, or long-distance shots taken from the safety of a surrounding moat, she could've gone to a zoo. Her goal was to get stunning close-ups and free-roaming action photos in a near natural habitat. And there was only one way to do it. *Faith.*

"I'm ready this time," she said calmly. "Let's bring Fang out to play."

Brand released the latch on the big cage and led Fang out into the forest clearing. Faline rubbed her hands across the fabric of Brand's cotton shirt, drawing comfort and security from it. She wasn't sure how the tiger would respond to the shirt-switching idea, but it was definitely helping her. She even remembered to breathe when Brand approached her, with Fang trotting curiously by his side.

Fang's great yellow-green eyes were gleaming at her, his head only a few feet away, the lithe muscles rippling beneath a shimmering coat of exquisite fur, striped and silky. He was an awe-inspiring sight, and so beautiful that Faline momentarily forgot her fear and put out a tentative hand to touch him. Fang responded by sniffing her suspiciously, his long whiskers tickling against her palm.

Faline didn't move or withdraw her hand. Brand was standing so close, with one arm protectively behind the tiger's head, she knew he was ready to intervene in case of trouble. She also knew it wouldn't be necessary. Something had changed inside her, and Fang was smart enough to sense it.

Her eyes met Brand's for an instant, and she smiled, then felt something wet and scratchy against the back of her hand. She looked down, laughing, as Fang proceeded to clean her with the damp surface of his sandpaper tongue.

"Thank you," she told the tiger gently, "but I've already had my shower this morning." She reached out with her other hand to scratch him hard behind the ear, the way she'd seen Brand do it.

Fang's reaction was even better than she'd hoped for. He dropped to the ground in front of her with a clumsy thud and rolled playfully onto his back, exposing the greater part of his body to the possibility of further petting.

Brand let out a low chuckle and chided the tiger for caving in so quickly under the influence of feminine wiles. "Not that I blame you, old boy," he added ruefully. "The lady's hard to resist. But try to maintain a little dignity at least. You *are* lord of the jungle."

Faline giggled and knelt down to stroke Fang softly under the chin. He tilted his head back and made a spluttering noise, a funny half-purr that Faline took as a sign of high praise.

Brand groaned in disgust. "Not a shred of pride left. He's going to start slobbering soon. Do you have this effect on every male you meet, Ms. Eastbrook?"

Faline flushed hotly, but she didn't answer. If only Brand knew what she felt for *him*. She kept her eyes riveted on Fang and tried to acknowledge the emotions to herself. Brand dropped to the ground beside them, distracting her as he held out a stick for the tiger to toy with. Fang's eyes focused immediately on the stick, and Faline's went involuntarily to Brand, to the magnificent male body clad only in blue jeans.

The physical attraction between them had been growing even stronger since the night by the swimming pool. But Faline suddenly realized that her emotions had become deeply involved as well.

He'd taught her something new about herself, encouraged her to risk again, shown her what the rewards could be. In a small way, she'd allowed herself to trust him, putting her physical safety entirely in his hands. He'd helped her to overcome her fear of the tiger. And although Fang was no longer a threat, she couldn't help feeling that her heart was still facing the greatest danger of all.

The danger of dropping her guard completely and letting Brand Weston inside. The danger of drowning in those deep amber eyes and never being free again.

She smiled as Brand and the tiger rolled over and over on the hard-packed ground, playing a fierce tug-of-war with the stick. She finally felt a part of it, but that was the scariest emotion yet.

Sooner or later, her time at the ranch would come to an end.

Brand finally won the battle and sent the stick flying for Fang to fetch, but the clever tiger wouldn't have any part of it. He lolled over to Faline, putting a paw gently against her shoulder, nuzzling his face in her hand. *Scratch here*, his expression said. *Just behind the ear*, *please.*

"Traitor!" Brand scolded, and propped himself up on one elbow, watching her tender ministration on the tiger with an expression close to envy.

Fang started spluttering again, oblivious to his master's apparent disgust.

Brand shook his head. "It's hopeless."

A voice sounded in the trees behind them, and a stranger approached, tall, tan, and dark-haired. "Surely not *hopeless*," he quipped, grinning at Brand. "Could be just a case of puppy love, or in this case, *kitty* love."

Brand groaned and let his head drop back to the ground. "Is that your best medical opinion, *Doctor* Ryder?"

Doc Ryder took a long, appreciative look at Faline and added, "My personal opinion as well. Can't blame Fang here for having good taste."

Fang, who was obviously well acquainted with the newcomer, sprawled out on the ground for a nap, but Brand's eyes narrowed at the comment, and he stood to shake his friend's hand. "No, we can't blame Fang. But I know your taste, Marshall, and I suggest you keep your opinions strictly professional."

Marshall raised a curious eyebrow, looking from Faline to Brand and back again, taking in every detail, from Brand's bare chest to Faline's strange choice of shirts. "Sure thing, buddy, but aren't you at least going to introduce me?"

"Faline Eastbrook," Brand said bluntly, motioning in her direction, "the photographer hired by *Eco*. Faline, meet Marshall Ryder. The local vet and a *friend* of mine."

Faline stood expectantly and held out her hand, laughing as he winked wickedly and raised her hand to his lips.

"Just to let you know we're not all uncivilized here in Winter Haven," he assured her, laying on the charm. "Some of us still know how to treat a lady."

"And some of us know how not to make asses of ourselves," Brand retorted dryly. "Did you come to check the panther or to practice your leer?"

"Can't I do both?" Marshall asked, ogling Faline with a look so lecherous, it started her laughing again.

Brand didn't look amused. "You can get the hell out of here unless you plan to practice that suggestive bedside manner somewhere else."

Marshall held a hand to his chest as though he'd been fatally wounded. "Suggestive! And I thought all along I was being suave. All right! I can tell Wildman Weston isn't in a joking mood. Let's go have a look at the panther before I wind up in need of medical attention myself."

Faline followed them to the cage, listening intently as they discussed the mother cat's recovery and the present condition of her cub. Brand held the panther in a remote neck harness as Marshall gingerly palpated the injured leg. With any wild creature, Brand explained, it was better to have as little human contact as possible. Growing too tame while in captivity could cause the panther harm when she had to readjust to her natural environment.

After watching her walk the length of the cage several times, Marshall finally pronounced her fit for reentry into the Everglades. It was time for the mom and her cub to be set free again in the only wilderness they'd ever known. Faline felt a little gloomy at the prospect.

She'd liked the panthers from the first day, finding it easier to adjust to their relatively small size and sleek beauty than to the restless ferocity of the lions. And compared to Fang, who was more than twice the mother's weight, the female panther was a real pussycat.

"A good photo opportunity," Marshall suggested innocently. "Why don't you take the lady along, Brand?"

"No doubt you'll be inviting yourself too."

Marshall frowned slightly, but the hint of humor never left his eyes. "Can't. Booked solid this week. A pig hernia, a diabetic poodle to pamper. You know how it is."

"Uh-huh," Brand responded.

"I'll fix the cat up with the radio collar," Marshall continued. "And square it all with the Panther Interagency Committee. They'll want to set someone up to track and monitor her movements for future study. I don't recommend tranquilizers. Could be too risky for the mother, but something tells me *you* could use some, Brand."

The Wildman kept stoically silent, but Marshall turned to Faline and suggested she bring along large quantities of mosquito repellent. "The Everglades are notorious for them," he explained. "And a sweet thing like you is liable to draw swarms."

She smiled. "Brand warned me about the insects around here, but so far they haven't been half as bad as I expected."

"The Glades are worse," Brand commented. "So you'd better dress carefully. Long sleeves, long pants, and sturdy shoes."

Faline's face brightened. "So you'll take me then?"

He nodded. "Like Ryder said, it's a photo opportunity and a chance to do the panthers some good. The more people who see them in *Eco*, the better."

"So when do we leave?" she asked eagerly.

"First thing in the morning," he told her.

"Pack your gear tonight. And don't forget to bring a change of clothes."

"Extra clothes?" Faline asked almost reluctantly. "You mean we'll be spending the night?"

Brand nodded, seemingly oblivious to her hesitation. "I'll see if I can find an extra sleeping bag for you."

"Sleeping bag?"

"Sure," he responded casually. "We'll be camping out."

Camping out, she repeated to her spinning brain. *With the Wildman. Alone.*

EIGHT

By the time the sun broke through the trees the next morning, Brand already had the panthers loaded in their covered cage in the back of his pickup. Mrs. Twitchford had arrived a little earlier than usual and was packing a cooler full of food for them to take on the long trip. Faline was the only one dragging her feet.

She hadn't slept well, and she couldn't decide what she'd need to bring with her. Insect repellent she had plenty of, but it wasn't the mosquitoes she was worried about.

"Let's get the show on the road, Ms. Eastbrook," he called to her from the foot of the stairs. "We've got a long drive ahead of us."

And a long night, Faline added silently, throwing the last of her clothes into her suitcase. But in the meantime there was a job to do, and a pair of panthers who needed their freedom. She grabbed the camera bag and headed downstairs.

Mrs. Twitchford relinquished the heavy cooler into Brand's arms and gave Faline a bracing hug. "Have a safe trip," she murmured.

Safe? Faline glanced speculatively at Brand over the older woman's shoulder. He was wearing a dark T-shirt, with slim-fitting blue jeans, a pair of cowboy boots, and a leather cord that caught the long golden hair in a rakish ponytail. Sighing, she realized the trip would be anything but that.

"Time to hit the road," he called as he walked out the front door and stowed the last of their luggage in the rear of the truck. After a final check on the panthers, he climbed into the cab and revved the engine impatiently. "You coming?" he asked finally, as Faline stood outside the passenger door, her feet fairly rooted to the ground. "Or have you caught a case of Twitchford's allergies?"

Faline forced herself to crawl into the seat next to him. It wasn't her allergies that were bothering her. It was her hormones.

Brand didn't wait for the final diagnosis. He gunned the engine, and they sped smoothly out the front gate, heading south.

"Pretty quiet today," he observed, after some time on the road without a peep from his normally talkative companion. She was especially skittish this morning. And he'd thought they'd made a lot of progress yesterday. The woman was harder to read than a pregnant leopard.

She glanced at him sideways. "Guess so. I didn't get much sleep."

Neither had he, for that matter. And the short time he had spent sleeping had been taken up with restless dreams. Dreams of a sweet, sensual woman who'd finally decided to share his bed. The night fantasies were slow and seductive.

"You feel okay?" he asked. She certainly looked fine. Really fine, he noted, even in the long sleeves he'd suggested. It had been a stupid idea after all, as though an extra few inches of fabric could stop what nature had already set in motion. As though some little pearl buttons could keep him from stripping her clothes off if he wanted to. God, how he wanted to.

So much for the instinct of self-preservation. His brain knew better than to get in too deep and risk another loss he couldn't handle. But the rest of him realized that the battle was basically over. He wanted to release her from the pain of the past. He wanted to make her his. He wanted to believe that the consequences would be worth it.

"I'm fine," she told him quietly, a telltale flush heightening the soft color of her cheeks.

He knew exactly what was ailing her, and sleeplessness was only a minor side effect. She had all the symptoms—the beautiful blush, the shallow breathing, the dilated pupils staring back at him from limpid green eyes. Involuntary mating signals, biologically designed to attract him. And doing a damn good job of it.

He gripped the steering wheel, fighting the urge to pull the truck off the road and show her just how right it could be between them. To show her the kinds of things that two people, uninhibited by fear and apprehension and uncertainty, could do.

"Take a nap," he suggested. "We still have a long way to go." And he still had a pair of panthers to take care of. His own needs and those of Ms. Eastbrook would have to wait until later.

Faline did feel her eyes growing heavy, her body being lulled by the gentle vibrations of the truck as it ate up the long stretch of blacktop road. The sun was beating down warmly on her through the windshield glass, and she shut her eyes against it, soaking up the rays as she snuggled close to the passenger side door. A nap sounded so delicious. It wouldn't hurt to close her eyes for just a few minutes.

"Wake up," Brand whispered against her ear.

She sighed heavily, cuddling closer to the comforting warmth against her face. "I *am* awake," she insisted drowsily, brushing away the persistent hand on her shoulder. "I was only resting my eyes for a minute. And it was your idea," she added, her brain a little hazy from the effects of the sun.

The hand nudged her again, harder this time, and she felt a warm, masculine breath, soft and caressing against her temples. "You've been resting your eyes for several hours now. And I'm not sure it was such a good idea. My shoulder's almost numb."

"Your shoulder?" she repeated, still groggy. Her eyes popped open. His shoulder! She'd been snuggling against him in her sleep, napping for *hours* with her head propped comfortably on his arm. No wonder she felt so good. But Lord, it was embarrassing. She couldn't even keep a respectable distance from him when she was unconscious.

"Sorry!" she said, scooting over to her side of the cab, sitting up to take a look around. "Oh!" she added momentarily, surprised that they had come to a complete stop by the side of the road. In the middle of nowhere. "Where are we?"

"Alligator Alley, at the north end of the Everglades. I thought you'd want to get your camera out before we go any farther. And it was getting a little tough to keep driving with you sleeping on my arm."

"Are you really numb?" she asked, guiltily.

"Just my shoulder. That's what makes it so tough."

The thump in the back of the pickup indicated that the panthers were ready to get on with the trip. As Brand got out to check on them, Faline took another cursory look around. And felt as though they were the last two people left on the face of the earth.

The four-lane highway cut a wide path through tall cypress trees and dense grassy lowlands. A large bird was perched on a massive nest of sticks overhead, topping a high wooden pole like a giant scarecrow having a bad hair day. Faline guessed the bird was an osprey, a local tidbit she'd picked up from her travel guide. She began to wonder if a basic survival manual might've been more useful.

Brand returned to the cab, popping the top on a can of cold soda, passing a second one to her. "In this kind of heat it's a good idea to drink plenty of liquids."

Faline followed suit, taking a long, refreshing swig. She was a lot less concerned about dehydration than she was about outdoor etiquette. Like where to go to the bathroom, for instance, when there wasn't a bathroom in sight.

"Brand," she began tentatively, pausing for the right words. "I don't suppose you know of a nice clean gas station nearby?"

He gave her a slow grin, rapped open the glove compartment with the back of his fist, and handed her a roll of toilet paper. "Pick your spot." He gestured to the wilderness around them.

Faline refused to give Brand the satisfaction of seeing her behave like some squeamish city girl. And she knew from the wicked look on his face that was exactly what he was expecting. She grabbed the roll from his hand without a single comment, and let herself out of the truck, considering her options.

Trees, bushes, or tall grass. Some choice! But it really didn't seem so important as it might have a week before. Her priorities had definitely begun to change. She didn't even miss her own bathroom with its almost-floor-length mirror and cracked pedestal sink. Still, some running water would've been nice. Not to mention the extravagance of a *toilet.*

She started walking toward the closest patch of trees, when she heard an amused voice call after her, "Watch out for snakes!"

After that welcome warning she proceeded at a more gingerly pace, but the only snake she encountered was the tall blond one sitting behind the wheel of the truck on her return. She put the roll carefully back in its place, grateful at least for small luxuries.

Another thump sounded in back.

"Everything okay back there?" she asked.

Brand nodded. "Mama's ready to leave real soon. I'd like to get a little deeper into her home range before we let them go. This highway is the one they were injured on."

As if to emphasize the impact of his words, a bright red Cadillac roared past them, kicking up a small cloud of sand in its wake.

"Plenty of people just ignore the speed limit," he said, shaking his head in disgust. "And even if they do see the cats, it's usually too late to stop by then. The animals don't even have a chance."

Faline felt the anger in his voice, and outrage welled up inside her. The panthers were too beautiful, too regal to die in such a senseless way. She was more determined than ever to get some dynamite pictures. It was the only way she knew how to help.

"Is that what all this fence is for?" she asked, pointing to the high metal chain link that spanned the length of the highway on either side.

"It helps," Brand said. "It's meant to keep the cats protected. Underpasses have been built beneath the road so the cats can cross it in safety, but animals have a strange way of not following all human directions. Some of them still get onto the highway. We can't fence in the whole tip of the state, but at this point, anything's worth a try. There are less than fifty panthers remaining in the wild."

Faline shook her head in frustration. "So what's the answer?"

"Preserve their habitat. It's the only hope the panthers have left, unless they're destined to live out the future as zoo specimens, bred and raised only in captivity. For my part, I prefer to see them in the wild."

Another thump from the mother panther seemed to prove that she was in total agreement.

They drove deeper into the grassy wetlands, taking a dirt access road that led into the heart of a hardwood hammock.

"We'll stop here," Brand announced after they'd bumped along the road for some time. "It's far enough from the main highway, and it'll give the mother some time to get acclimated to her surroundings before dark. She's nocturnal by nature, but has had to readjust her schedule slightly since recuperating in captivity."

Faline grabbed her camera bag, selecting her lens carefully as Brand unloaded the great cage from the pickup, sliding it gently down a sturdy wooden ramp. Both panthers looked eager to leave, pacing restlessly behind the confines of the steel bars. Faline felt the excitement mounting, almost believing that it was she instead of the panthers who was about to be given the gift of freedom.

Brand's hand was on the latch, ready to slide the door open at any minute but he was relaxed, waiting patiently for her to signal him with a thumbs-up.

"If she gets ornery," he warned, "don't take any stupid chances, just get your butt inside the truck, pronto, understand?"

She wet her lips, nodding but unafraid. She checked the f-stop setting one more time and held the camera poised for action. "Ready."

As soon as Brand had worked the door open, the mother panther slipped out, sniffing curiously at the air around her. She hesitated, then looked back, encouraging her cub to follow. Faline set the camera instantly in motion, the high-speed shutter whirring away to capture the animal's every expression.

The little cub didn't need too much coaxing from his mother, and he bounded out quickly, padding behind her on oversize paws. Faline snapped several shots of his receding behind, and the little tail that moved like quicksilver, but she was hoping that he would turn around for a last look. As if sensing Faline's thoughts, Brand called softly to the mother, and the sleek cat rewarded him with a final glance before disappearing into the tall grass.

The cub hesitated a moment longer, and Faline quietly kissed the air, still hopeful. He looked around at her, and stood still as a statue, his head cocked curiously to one side. Faline held her breath and snapped the shutter, capturing the most emotional moment of her career, and saving the priceless face forever on film.

A second later, the little guy tumbled off into the grass, following his mother for parts unknown. Gone! And it had only taken an instant.

Faline's heart was in her throat, and she swallowed hard, turning to Brand. "That's it," she whispered, teary-eyed in spite of her vow not to go all mushy in front of him.

But he didn't seem to mind. He walked over and put his arms around her, strong and comforting. "Hush, Wildcat. You're too tough to cry, remember?"

She sniffed indignantly, burying her face in his chest. "Tough, not *heartless*," she mumbled into his T-shirt. She tipped her head back to look into his eyes. "How could you let them go like that and not feel something?"

He wiped her eyes with the hem of his shirt and led her to the back of the truck, kicking the ramp away. He lifted her up to sit on the trailing metal edge and leaned against it. "I do feel something, but I've learned to deal with it my own way. I try to remember that the panthers were never mine to begin with. They were just passing through for a while, and that's what I told myself every day they were with me. Just passing through."

Faline felt her heart constricting at the phrase. Was that how he saw her as well? As another wild thing that was just passing through his life? And it was true after all, wasn't it? She didn't have any hope of staying. Or did she?

"And you like it that way?" she asked softly.

He gave her a lazy smile, the kind that sent skyrockets shooting through her. "I didn't say I liked it. It just makes the good-bye easier to take."

She searched his amber eyes for a deeper answer, for the one that could help her to understand. "But don't you just want to hold on sometimes? To hold on hard and never let go?"

He shook his head gently. "When I was younger, I thought I could control the outcome by trying to hang on. It took me a long time to realize it just doesn't work that way. Every living being has its own free will. The tighter your grip on them, the more they struggle for release and freedom. The wisdom comes when you learn to loosen your hold and let them live the way they were meant to. When you learn that, control is just an illusion and relinquishing it is where the real power lies."

Faline thought she understood him on some level. He was telling her that the rewards came from letting go. That it was far more painful to try and master what was ultimately beyond your control. She knew the words were true. She simply wasn't sure she had the strength to use it.

She closed her eyes, conjuring up the image of the panthers again, remembering the last adorable look on the cub's curious face. Even if it had been tough to see them go, she wouldn't have traded that moment for anything. It was a memory to savor.

The sun was fading to pink, casting streams of rose and gold across the grasses, silhouetting the tall cypresses against the evening sky like dark arrows shot to the ground from heaven. Faline blinked at the beauty of it, a world transformed by light and the approaching mystery of the night. The grasses seemed to come alive around them, golden slivers of tinsel rustling gently from a faraway ocean breeze, rippling and whispering in an exotic language she could almost comprehend.

Her gaze drifted back to Brand. Their eyes met in mutual understanding.

"We'd better make camp," he said brusquely. "When it gets dark out here, it gets *very* dark. And the dry grasses make a campfire too big a risk."

They rolled the sleeping bags out on a patch of dry ground and ate a cold alfresco supper as the brilliant show of the painted sunset played above them. Faline held her breath as the last stripe of vibrant purple shimmered over the horizon, then faded to midnight-blue. A stunning attraction the travel guide had failed to mention.

Nor had it mentioned anything about surviving an evening alone with Wildman Weston. It'd been different sleeping in his house. Houses had marvelous modern conveniences like walls and doors. Doors with locks. But here—here they were not only alone, and in as remote an area as she could've imagined, but her only hope at privacy was the plastic zipper on a flimsy sleeping bag.

A few days ago she would've traded her enlarger for a chance to be alone with him. For another chance at what they'd shared in the backyard by the pool. But the primitive reality of the wilderness, combined with the feeling that they were the last two people left on earth, had made her lose her nerve.

There was no telling what might happen in a situation like this. A slightly jittery woman. A virile wildman. A dark night. She shivered, hugging her arms to her chest.

"Cold? It must be over seventy degrees tonight."

Faline shrugged. "Guess I have thin blood or something."

"Or something," he agreed, drawing closer to sit cross-legged beside her on the sandy ground.

"Here, I'll warm you up." He laid a hand at the back of her neck.

Faline jumped as though an electric jolt had shot through her.

"Touchy, aren't we?"

She shook her head, casting a quick, wishful glance at her sleeping bag. "Maybe I'd better turn in."

There was a long pause. "If that's what you want."

She bit her lower lip, trying to decide exactly what she did want. The cautious, sensible part of her wanted to scramble into the bag at top speed and pull the zipper securely shut, locking in every vulnerable inch of her body from the tip of her toes to the top of her head. The other half of her wanted to invite Brand in beside her and see what would happen when he was given free rein. Who was she kidding? She knew what would happen.

"We could zip the bags together," he suggested casually. "They're made that way. To fit each other perfectly."

"Oh. Were you thinking about going to sleep now too?"

"To be honest, I wasn't."

Her heart went a little crazy, her breathing quickening painfully as she thought about what Brand had in mind. But then, she hadn't exactly been contemplating sleep herself. "I guess singing camp songs is out of the question."

"I'm not much of a Boy Scout, Faline," he responded softly.

"And roasting marshmallows could be tough without a fire," she murmured.

"We don't have to do anything," he said quietly. "Nothing's going to happen here, unless you'd like it to."

She brushed back a smooth strand of hair that had strayed against her lashes. "And suppose I would like it to? What then?"

Brand watched the flush of innocent awareness stealing across her face, making her more beautiful, more tempting than he'd thought possible. He was bewitched, beguiled. She made him feel as predatory as Fang, as animal as the male lion when the females were in heat. His body was burning like fire and brimstone, hot with carnal instinct, driven with the desire to mate. He'd already chosen his partner. The one female that could satisfy him. She would have to make the final choice.

"Then you tell me what you want," he said.

She hesitated, unconsciously wetting her lower lip with the tip of her tongue. "Can we start off slow?"

Slow? Brand studied the way her mouth had parted, her lips wet and seductive. The sight nearly knocked the wind out of him. Hell, he'd do it any way she wanted. But it was bound to be an evening of sweet, tender agony.

"Wildcat, we can take all night."

All night. Faline definitely didn't know if her

heart would last that long. Her pulse was throbbing in her ears, radiating warmth to every tender part of her body. She felt dizzy, almost faint, and mesmerized by Brand's golden gaze.

As if to prove the promise of his words, he tucked a hand under her chin and tilted her face up toward him, softly stroking her cheek. His touch was one of unexpected tenderness, light, sensuous, seductive. Faline felt herself melting under the long leisurely caresses, dissolving into the slow stimulation.

Before she fully realized what was happening, she was caught up in his arms, cradled against the hard expanse of his chest. Her legs were stretched out on the sandy ground, her face only inches away from the warmth of his mouth. He was murmuring something in her ear, the words were sweet, secretive, exciting.

"Nice and slow," he whispered. "Is that how you like it?"

She looked up at him, his eyes reflecting an emotion she was afraid to name. Her heart tightened in her chest, then swelled as his hot, tender glance forced the air from her lungs in a shuddering sigh. His strokes grew bolder, as his hands worked their way down her neck, his palms possessively splaying across the thin fabric of her blouse.

His touch tightened rhythmically, his fingers exploring insistently against the tender tips of her breasts. The warmth of his hands spread through her, sending tiny shocks of desire tingling down every nerve. A sweet pain lanced to the base of her spine as he moved one hand up under her blouse, pushing back the stiff lace of her bra, massaging her nipples into full, overflowing arousal.

His head dropped to her chest, the long mass of golden hair falling against her soft, sex-warmed skin as he fitted his mouth to her breast. Faline ran her fingers through the sensuous, silky waves, clutching him to her as his tongue explored her most sensitive areas, his teeth nipping gently. She let out an involuntary whimper, the pleasure so intense, it was almost painful, the stimulation nearly too much to take.

Did he realize what he was doing to her? she wondered. Did he know that he'd started a slow burn deep in her belly, an aching fire that was spreading to every limb, scorching her with sensation? Did he understand that no man had ever drawn those feelings from her before?

When he pulled back to look at her, his eyes told her that he knew it all. Knew that she was nearly ready to risk again, to let go. He knew what it meant to her, understood every sharp stirring, every craving that he'd given her. The look on his face said he planned to give her more.

Brand studied her, the softly flushed face, the wide-eyed look. The signs were all there. Faline was ready, ripe for the taking. But he wouldn't take her just yet. He wanted to pleasure her slowly, surely.

He'd moved too fast that night by the pool,

scared her with the intensity of his own need. He wouldn't make the same mistake twice. Tonight he would make it long and languorous. Erotic, teasing torture.

He would keep the need inside him at bay until her desire matched his own. And he wouldn't take her until she begged him for release.

But dear Lord, her breasts felt good to his touch. Soft, full, and silken. Like cream ambrosia, sweet, ripe, and sensual. He wanted to devour every delicate, delicious part of her.

His groin muscles tightened at the thought, gripping painfully as though someone had knocked the wind right out of him. It made him hard just thinking about her that way. The woman was built for pleasure. For *his* pleasure. But she would probably make him die of desire before he took it. He smiled slowly to himself, vowing to return the favor.

NINE

Brand felt a low throb course through him, a pulse of pleasure at the thought of the long night ahead. There were liberties he wanted to take with Faline, liberties he knew she was finally willing to allow. Her heart, her head, were finally ready to let it happen. Now he only needed to help the rest of her get ready.

There were ways to make a woman weak with pleasure, abandoned acts of love a wildman knew instinctively. A look, a sound, a touch could heighten sexual responsiveness, drive a woman to distraction. And Faline was the most incredibly responsive woman he'd ever met. The combination promised to be soul-shattering.

For both of them.

He dipped his head toward her lips, ready for the taste of passion.

"Ouch!"

He stopped, a little confused. *Ouch?* Definitely *not* the response he was expecting.

"Ow!" Faline slapped frantically at the base of her bare ankles. "Something's biting me!"

Brand swore softly, cursing the tropical climate. Insects were encroaching on his territory, attacking the tender body that only he had a right to. If any creature devoured Faline tonight, he was damn sure it was going to be him.

"Mosquitoes, maybe," he speculated. "Or sand fleas." It was too dark to tell.

"Fleas?" she squeaked in a horrified voice.

"Don't get squeamish. They're not the kind that come home to live with you. But they're a bloody nuisance around here at night." He slapped the back of his neck, feeling an irritating sting. Nasty little things. But he was prepared for them. Maybe there was a bit of the Boy Scout left in him after all.

"Insect repellent!" Faline suggested, reading his mind.

"There's a can in the glove compartment." He eased himself out from under her. "Sit tight. I'll take care of them."

He retrieved the can at top speed, feeling more predatory than ever. Modern science was a wonderful thing, lifting man above the lesser beasts. Contemporary savages didn't have to be at the mercy of bloodthirsty bugs.

"Stand up," he told her calmly. "I'll lather you

down." A few squirts of this stuff and they'd be back in business.

Faline stood obligingly, her back toward him, lifting the hair from behind her neck. Brand started there, pumping the fluid onto the skin at her throat, her hands, up her blouse, and down around the tempting curve of her ankles. Then he quickly doused his own body in the liquid.

"Ow! I think they're still biting."

He felt a vicious jab on his arm, and realized she wasn't kidding. The flying pests were dive-bombing at both of them, with greater enthusiasm than ever.

"What the—" He suddenly got a whiff of himself and realized what was happening. He'd just covered the both of them with suntan lotion. Sweet, sticky, coconut-scented lotion. And the bugs were loving every bit of it, eating them alive.

He slapped hard as one dark, determined speck landed on his throat and started pricking his flesh with the voracity of a vampire.

"Sorry, Faline. Guess I grabbed the wrong stuff." He wanted to add that some of the responsibility was hers. How was he supposed to read labels when his brain was occupied with other thoughts? Graphic, gut-wrenching thoughts. Thoughts that spurred him back to the truck, to retrieve the correct can. Just to be on the safe side, he double-checked the label in the moonlight. Bugs-be-Gone. That was it. Great stuff.

Faline was still slapping every few seconds, dancing and darting to avoid the swarming hoard.

"One more time, baby. Turn around."

He performed the ritual for the second time, re-covering every exposed area he could find. He drenched both of them in it, and by the time he'd finished, the insects had retreated into the swamp. And the two of them were left standing in a cloud of spray that reeked something fierce.

"Feel anything?" he asked cautiously.

"No, but it smells *awful.* No wonder the bugs don't like it."

"It'll wear off," he said doubtfully.

"Peel off is more like it. Did you have to use the whole can?"

"What do you want? I stopped them, didn't I?"

"You *drowned* them." She sank down onto the ground, trying in vain to wipe some of the excess onto the grass.

Brand silently cursed the cruelties of fate. There was nothing like the wilderness to put a woman in the mood. And nothing like the odor of ripe coconut and Bugs-be-Gone to get her out of it. He couldn't blame her, really. It was hard to think about lovemaking when you smelled like a poison piña colada.

But he was still thinking about it. Which either meant that he really was an uncivilized savage, or Faline was the most exciting, irresistible woman he'd ever known.

He dropped down beside her and tore off his

T-shirt, rubbing it gently across the exposed surface of her arms and ankles. The cloth soaked up some of the surplus spray, but the ground presented them with an entirely new problem. *Sand.* It was clinging to the sticky surface of their skin like wet, scratchy cement.

Faline's eyes flew to the bare expanse of Brand's chest. God, did he have to torture her like that? It was bad enough to be excited to the point of pain and have a bunch of sadistic insects interrupt what promised to be an incredible night of passion. But flaunting that magnificent body in front of her was cruel and unusual punishment. Sheer, sexual torture. It almost hurt to look at him.

A sweet pain shot through her body, but the most compelling awareness was the way her flesh responded to the sight of him. She was conscious of an ache in her nipples, a slow heat between her legs, and the realization that she still wanted him. Smelly, gritty, here in the dirt, it didn't matter how. The cautious city girl was gone. She was a woman in need. And Brand was the only male who could ease her desire.

"Brand—" She stopped, aware of his eyes upon her. They were burning in the darkness, with a bright intensity that matched her own.

"Tell me what you want, Wildcat."

"I want—" She was just about to say it, when she felt a new sensation around her ankles. Something small and ticklish crawling on her legs. "Ants!" Faline slapped at her feet until she rid herself of the last crawling pest. Then she grabbed her sleeping bag, giving it a sound shake. If a nest of scorpions had fallen out, she wouldn't have been a bit surprised. But it was mercifully free of bugs, and she searched for a safe patch of ground to lay it on.

"It's no use," Brand said, casting his eyes heavenward. "We're in for some rain."

Faline didn't doubt it for a second. She couldn't decide whether to laugh or cry. Brand stood to put his arm around her and led her to the enclosed cab of the truck. He opened the door and settled her inside, rubbing a hand across her cheek. "You'll be more comfortable in here tonight," he told her. "No bugs. No rain. I'll sack out in the back."

"We could still zip the bags together," she suggested softly.

He let out a low groan. "Have mercy on me, woman. No way would I get any sleep."

Faline sighed and snuggled herself into the bag as Brand shut the door behind her. It was a far cry from a hotel, but the safety of the bug-free cab was a welcome refuge. Brand wasn't only the sexiest man alive, he was also the most considerate. She closed her eyes, giving in to the exhaustion, hoping that her body might find some physical release in sleep.

Brand grabbed a small whiskey flask from the cooler and zipped himself into his bag just as the rain started to fall. He swore virulently and tossed back a comforting shot of the fiery liquid. The whiskey burned a slow path down his throat and eased a little of the aching in his belly, but he knew the whole bottle wouldn't be enough to tamp down the painful remnants of desire. He cast a hungry glance inside the cab of the truck. The cure for that particular ailment would have to wait.

He ducked his head down out of the drizzling rain and savagely recapped the flask. One swig was all he'd allow himself. The mosquitoes were still lurking out there in the dark, and if they decided to resume their bloodsucking assault, he damn well wouldn't provide them the pleasure of intoxication.

He closed his eyes, praying for an early sunrise.

The drive back to the ranch seemed interminable to Faline, who would've traded her best telephoto lens for ten minutes in a hot shower. She'd managed to comb the tangles from her hair and splash some bottled water on her face, but the rest of her remained hot, sticky, and disheveled. She slipped on a pair of dark glasses and leaned against the passenger side door, grateful for the noise on the radio. At least Brand didn't expect her to make polite small talk. Maybe his minimalist manners weren't so savage after all.

As soon as they'd pulled the truck up to the house, Faline escaped inside, half hoping to see the sympathetic Mrs. Twitchford waiting for her with open, comforting arms. But she regretfully remembered that it was the housekeeper's day off and ran upstairs, making a beeline for the shower. Never again would she take the luxury of running water for granted. It was going to be pure, sensuous ecstasy.

She stripped her clothes off, vowing to burn the smell out of them if necessary, and stepped eagerly under the soothing, streaming jets. She sighed blissfully, letting the liquid warmth steal over her, running in languorous, muscle-relaxing rivulets from the top of her hair down to the curling tips of her toes. Nothing had ever felt so good. Nothing except . . .

She ran slippery hands over her naked body, remembering the feel of Brand's touch against her taut, burning skin. His hands had been tender, rough, and thrilling. Her heart squeezed and tightened as she remembered how slowly and skillfully he'd handled her.

Faline realized that his darkest male desire lay just below the surface, lurking somewhere within him. The savage, primitive part of him was still there, waiting. Waiting for the female who was daring enough to set it free.

Waiting for her. But was she ready to take the risk? She had been last night. If the surroundings had been different, she doubted she'd be worrying about it now. More than likely she'd still be in his arms. Exactly where she wanted to be.

But how could she be sure the choice was right?

Her mind went back to what Brand had taught her about faith and trust and letting go. He'd never pushed her. He'd always been there when she'd needed him most—with the photography, with Fang, with sending the panthers away. He'd always made it clear that the choice was hers.

Faline worked the soap into a thick, creamy lather, smoothing it carefully over every inch of her body. The experience was slow, voluptuous, delicate. For the first time, she was seeing her body in a whole new light. She understood the kind of pleasure it could bring to a man. It was a gift to share, to be given selectively, exclusively to the right man. To Brand Weston.

Brand himself was trying to cool off in the backyard pool, with Fang for a swimming companion. The tiger loved the water and was a powerful swimmer, but this afternoon he gravitated to his favorite spot in the shallow end, resting on the lower steps with all but his head and shoulders submerged.

Brand circled slowly in the deep end, careful not to splash any water in Fang's direction. The big cat invariably became irritated if his face got wet. And Brand wasn't about to provoke him. He was too busy trying to calm down himself.

The pool helped somewhat, the tepid water easing the warm fire under his skin, but it was a temporary solution at best. The burning deep within him wouldn't be damped by such paltry measures. The aching need wouldn't ease until he was deep within *her*.

He kicked onto his back, letting the water lap around him, and glanced up at the house. Faline was inside, he knew, alone in her bedroom, maybe hurting as badly as he was. Last night she'd been about to open up to him, about to let her guard down and trust him. She'd been so close to saying it. God, how he'd wanted her to say it, to ask him to make love to her.

He could sense it in her voice, in her scent, in the way she held herself, the tension of her body. She was just as crazy with need as he was. Extremely aroused, she was almost irresistible. *Almost.* He'd managed to resist so far. To wait until she came to him. But Lord, how long was it going to take?

He shook the water from his hair and climbed out of the pool, drawn to the house by his own cruel curiosity. Wrapping a towel around his waist, he settled Fang down for the night and went in search of some contentment for himself. Inside, he mounted the stairs two at a time and stopped outside Faline's room. Her door was open, but the bathroom was shut tight, and he heard the sound of running water inside.

He smiled to himself. Of course, she had wanted a shower. The bug spray had to go sooner or later. And the thought of her scrubbing it off was a pleasant one. Hell, it was more than pleasant, it was downright fascinating.

Steam was escaping through the cracks in the door, teasing him with long tendrils of misty scent, beckoning him to enter. Faline was naked behind that door, naked and wet and smelling of clean soap. Smelling fresh and innocent and sexual.

Brand's groin muscles tightened, and he froze at the threshold of her bedroom door. So much for the salubrious effects of the swimming pool. A few minutes out of the water and just the thought of her was making him hard again. He'd never known a woman who could excite him so quickly and thoroughly. He urged to claim her as his own, to take that dripping, steam-warmed body and possess it fully, sexually, spiritually, in every way he could imagine.

The low pulse within him grew stronger as he stepped inside the bedroom, walked to the bathroom door, and put his hand on the knob. And stopped.

His body was burning, but he was more man than animal, more thought and reason than primal impulse. The cognitive part of his brain was still in control, and it told him that to have Faline, body and spirit, she must come to him.

He would have to wait awhile longer, maybe forever, but he didn't want her any other way. His need for her went far beyond the physical now. He wanted her courage, her passion, her pure emotional surrender, or he wanted nothing at all.

And if she gave it by choice, it would only make their loving that much sweeter. He hesitated, then headed for his own bedroom.

Faline turned off the jets of water overhead and wrapped a towel around her freshly bathed body, reveling in the feel of delicious cleanliness. She finally smelled like herself again. As for the way she felt—she rubbed the moisture from a patch of steam-clouded mirror and peered curiously at her own reflection. There was something different in the wide green eyes staring back at her, a look of expectation she'd never seen there before.

Her body was waiting for something. Or someone. She saw it in the fullness of her lips, in the flushed intensity of her face, in the swelling softness of her breasts.

She knew it instinctively and understood perfectly now what she had to do. She had to let herself take a risk again. She had to go to Brand, to trust in herself again, to allow herself to trust in him.

She had to have faith, the kind he'd helped her to have with Fang. This time, she didn't need his help. She already knew the most intimate, most symbolic way to show it.

She dressed hurriedly, almost frantically, pulling on a satin bra and panties, covering herself with a matching satin robe. Dressing herself so he might have the pleasure of undressing her again soon. Very soon, if his need was half as urgent as hers.

She ran a comb through hair that was still damp, but the pressing desire within her wouldn't wait for more. Still in bare feet, still warm and a little wet, she walked down the hall to his room. Dusk was settling slowly, and she heard the lions calling in the woods outside, restless, uncaged, roaring in anticipation. Faline didn't bother to knock. She didn't want to lose her nerve, so she simply pushed the door open and walked inside.

Brand was standing by the window, looking down at the animals, but he turned in an instant and met her eyes. His hair was almost as damp as hers, combed boldly back from his forehead in long water-darkened waves. The muscles in his bare chest rippled as he crossed his arms in front of him and repositioned his jean-clad legs against the windowsill, watchful.

"I told you once this room was off-limits," he reminded her. "Don't come in unless you plan to stay. All night."

She took another step forward and watched the desire flare in his eyes. She knew the power of what she was doing. As well as the risk.

"This isn't a game we're playing, Faline. If it was, we both know who'd win."

She turned to pull the door shut, locking herself inside the room, making her decision final. This was it. She'd lain herself open, crossed the last line. Simply taking that step she knew a sense of strength and satisfaction.

She lifted her chin and met his gaze. "You also told me to say what I want. I want this."

The low groan he made was full of fever and relief, heavy with heat. Faline's heart went wild. There was no going back. There was only the night and the vibrancy inside her, and Brand to share it with.

"And *how* do you want it?" he asked, crossing the room to stand in front of her. "Nice and polite?" He brushed his fingertips against the silky sleeves of her robe. "Would you like me to say, 'Please'?"

Faline shook her head, but her throat was too tight to speak. Instead, she untied the belt on her robe and let the satin garment fall to the floor. Cool evening air caressed her damp skin as she trembled under Brand's burning stare.

"*Please*," he whispered, his voice hoarse and rusty. "Please don't do that unless you want a savage on your hands."

She fingered the thin strap of her bra and watched his eyes melt to molten amber. She knew it was reckless, crazy, the most daring thing she'd ever done, but at the same time she trusted him with her life. Wildman Weston was only part savage. The other part of him was passionate, protective male. And she *did* want him on her hands. On her hands, her body and inside every tight, aching part of her.

She pulled the strap down slowly, sighing with sensation as her breast overflowed from the silken edges of her bra. She heard Brand's breath catch in his throat. She reached up to drag the other strap down and peeled the second cup back, displaying herself openly to his burning eyes.

"Faline," he said thickly, "you are one dangerous woman. Beautiful, but dangerous."

She felt a quick, dizzy thrill at the words and reached back to undo the clasp on her bra. But as soon as the wispy garment drifted to the floor, Brand took a sudden step toward her, pinning her arms behind her. He backed her up against the door and let his eyes drop to the crested swells of her nipples, to the bare midriff beneath, and down to her satin panties.

"Beautiful," he repeated. "Will you *please* show me the rest?" As if to emphasize the meaning of his words, he kept her arms locked behind her and with his free hand, traced the line of her underwear with gentle, exploratory fingers.

Faline shivered with excitement and anticipation as his hand stroked and teased against her sensitive, straining flesh. He released her hands suddenly, and she dropped them to her panties, toying nervously with the lacy edge. Brand's hands closed over hers, strong, urgent, supportive. Together they began to pull the panties down.

The satin fell away in a small flimsy pile, and Faline stood naked and shaky in front of him. But he still had most of his clothes on. Well, jeans at least.

"You're next," she said boldly, reaching for the button at his waistband. She brazenly popped it open, and realized with a quick gasp that he wasn't wearing anything underneath. The Wildman was shamelessly undomesticated.

Instead of underwear, she discovered a dark, thrilling triangle of hair that jutted down to meet sex-hardened flesh, a massive male erection. She flashed back to the night by the pool, remembering how beautiful he'd looked. How big and beautiful. Tonight he seemed twice as large, and incredibly aroused. Suddenly she wasn't feeling quite so bold.

She sank back against the door, wondering what that masculine hardness was going to do to her. A vivid picture came quickly to mind, and a sharp thrill of fear shot through her. She wasn't sure if her body could take it. She wasn't even sure if it would all fit.

"You okay, Faline?" he asked quietly. "Don't go skittish on me now."

She shook her head, fighting for air. Skittish? Her main goal at the moment was to stay conscious.

He brushed back a damp strand of hair from her face, his fingers gentle and caressing against the velvet warmth of her cheek. "We can stop right now if you want. You don't have to go through with it."

When Brand considered the full impact of that

statement, he realized how bad he had it for Faline. Either that or the bugs had given him a serious case of brain fever. No matter that he wouldn't be able to walk for a week. He wasn't going to push her into something she wasn't prepared for. But God, he'd been primed for her all his life.

When she didn't answer immediately, he said, "Guess you're not ready."

She blinked up at him, anxious, eager. "I *want* to go through with it. I want you to *make* me ready."

His eyes darkened at the thought. It was an invitation, a challenge that no man could resist. This time he wouldn't go too fast for her. This time he would take her with him. Every slow, mind-shattering step of the way.

He let his jeans slide casually to the hardwood floor, stepped out of them, and took her firmly by the arm. "Turn around for me, Wildcat."

She followed his direction, a little afraid, but more than a little excited. She'd seen him rough, she'd seen him tender. Tonight she wanted him to be both.

She felt an alarming shock as he pulled her against him, her back locked tightly to his chest, the hardest part of him pressed provocatively at the base of her spine. All at once he was nuzzling the nape of her neck with his mouth, while his hands skillfully and rhythmically caressed the bare swells of her breasts.

She whimpered and dropped her head back

against his chest, writhing in pleasure as the rough friction of his fingers teased the tips of her nipples, intoxicating her with pure physical delight. His mouth drifted to the tender edge of her ear, nipping and biting at the base of her lobe, murmuring and coaxing in a coarse, evocative whisper. She clutched at the sides of his hips for support, pressing herself into him, and she heard him moan, the sound low and guttural.

"Woman," he breathed, "keep that up and I promise there's going to be trouble."

She locked her hips tighter to his body. "Promises, promises."

He swore softly and glided one palm to the base of her belly, nestling his fingers in the soft, satiny sweetness between her legs. Faline stifled a gasp as he probed and pleasured her in a slow circular motion. She couldn't believe he was touching her there. She couldn't believe how intensely, almost painfully good it felt.

The sensation was searing, hot, explosive, sending shafts of delight piercing right through her. Brand's gift for reading her reactions was intuitive, incredible, the most intimate kind of connection she'd ever known. He seemed to understand every tremor, every sigh, every slight sign of ecstasy within her, even though she hadn't uttered a word. It was as if he knew her body better than she did. He knew exactly what to do and exactly where to do it.

Faline went warm and achy within, sighing

blissfully at the shocking insistence of his touch. She was melting in his arms, her insides liquefying into a slippery puddle of pleasure. His arousal was pushed erotically against the sensitive underside of her buttocks. The thought of taking it all inside her didn't worry her anymore. Lord, she *wanted* it inside her, every hard, masculine inch of him.

She felt his knee push between her legs, spreading them apart, opening her to take more of the mind-blowing pressure from his bold fingertips. The tender battering on her nerves continued as he petted and teased, drawing sheer, ecstatic sensation from her with the sweet, forbidden stroking. Then he eased her legs a little wider and started to touch her in the sweetest, most shocking way imaginable.

Faline's muscles pulled hard inside, the pleasure so intense, she could hardly bear it. She started to move with the rhythm of the strokes, the steady beat of his hand compelling her to quick urgency.

"Good, baby," he whispered, his breath warm and languid against her ear. "It's gonna be so good between us."

Brand vaguely realized that had to be the understatement of the year. It was sweet heaven already.

The rocking of her body against him sent a violent shaft of excitement to the base of his groin. The hunger rose within him, clutching like a fist at his hot spot. Faline was all innocent sensuality, all delicate sexual desire. She was slick and wet and ready for him, so impetuous and uninhibited, it made his muscles knot from wanting her. Every fragile, feminine part of her.

He picked her up and carried her to the bed, laying her flat on her back. A muscle tightened in his jaw as she stared up at him, so sweet and wanting and almost his. He felt a sharp need driving him forward, a quick pulsing in his blood that he couldn't control much longer.

She arched her back as he moved over her, offering him the pinkest, most inviting breasts he'd ever seen, the nipples so lush and full, he couldn't keep himself from tasting them. He nibbled tenderly, tracing the dark, peaking centers with the length of his tongue, taking them full in his mouth, suckling each one in turn as she writhed and moaned with pleasure.

The sound excited him like crazy. *She* excited him like crazy. She was restless, unrestrained, and so seductively abandoned that every last shred of her caution had disappeared. Faline was even wilder than he'd imagined.

She reached out a delicate hand and slipped her fingers around the blood-filled base of his shaft, palming downward. The effect was excruciating, electric torture. He was too aroused, too hard for her to experiment like that. It was pain and elation mixed together, rapture and torment focused in one agonizing area. He groaned, his muscles straining and tightening.

She stopped. "Don't you—want me to?"

"Faline, let me show you what I want."

She made a soft sound of delight in his ear. "Yes, please."

He repositioned himself, poised at the opening between her legs. He thrust gently, afraid he might hurt her. She was so tender and tight, yet so moist and ready, that easing slowly into her took all of his self-control. He was halfway to paradise and still only partially inside her.

He pushed again, sinking deeper into wet satin, deeper into damp, bewitching bliss. She gasped, and her eyes fluttered open, surprised, frantic with excitement.

He bent to cover her face with light kisses. "Easy. You're so tight, I'm not all the way there yet."

She spread her legs wider, trying to accommodate the rest of him, and he thrust again, harder, until he realized it wasn't going to work. Not this way. Not when she was wound up so tightly with need. He'd nearly touched bottom, and if he went any farther, he was bound to hurt her.

"Relax, baby," he said, withdrawing, his jaw clenched hard.

She squirmed under him, clutching at his back in frustration. "*Please!*" she cried, her voice soft and shaky. "Please make love to me."

"It's gonna be fine," he said, stroking her shoulders, gentling her in his arms. "So fine. But we have to use a different position." He rolled over, pulling her on top of him. "Let's try it like this."

Her eyes grew wider, a little unsure. She wasn't as experienced as she was eager to please. She'd probably never given pleasure to a man this way before. The thought that she would share it with him for the first time was a humbling one. It was the greatest gift of trust she could have given him. She was willing to make the last leap of faith, no matter what. His heart squeezed tight in his chest, full of an emotion he couldn't name. He wanted to make it right for her. Never had anything felt so right for him.

"Come on," he coaxed. "You can do it, baby. We're almost there. Just go with whatever feels good." He didn't doubt that she could take more of him this way. And if she was in control, she wouldn't feel any pain.

Straddled on top of him, Faline felt the warmest part of her pressed against his groin. She closed her eyes, wondering just how to please him. *Just go with whatever feels good.* She'd try. She wanted to try, but she didn't want to disappoint him. And at the moment, everything about him felt good.

The hard, muscled heat of him, the smooth, sinewy flesh. She opened her eyes and looked down at his beautiful face. He was so handsome, so primitively perfect, and so concerned about her pleasure that her throat went tight.

He'd given her so much. He'd been so patient,

so protective. She knew on some level, this had to be a risk for him, too, but he'd never worried about protecting himself. She wanted to give back to him. For the first time in her life she wanted to make love in the most perfect sense.

She leaned forward to kiss him, tentatively at first, then deeper as his mouth opened to meet her tongue in a touch more intimate than any they had shared before. The taste of him drenched her in need, made her slick with desire. His hands moved up to massage her breasts, and her inhibitions were gone again. She was a woman set free.

She lifted up a little, rotating her hips, and eased the length of him into her. Her head fell back in sweet abandon as her most sensitive parts throbbed with pleasure. She raised up again and drove down harder, taking him in even deeper than before. But it wasn't enough. She was dying with need. She wanted to feel him move inside her. She wanted to feel the full, hot friction of it.

And just when she was ready to cry out in frustration, Brand braced his hands at the back of her buttocks and showed her the fastest way to heaven. He was thrusting inside her, rocking her slowly from side to side, back and forth. She followed his lead, moving her hips in a small, seductive circle, every hard inch of him in full, carnal contact with every soft part of her.

The combination was explosive.

Faline began to peak before she knew what was

happening, shuddering from the wild ecstasy of her own release.

Brand felt her starting to climax on top of him, and the sound of her joyful scream sent him over the edge. He wrapped her legs around him and rolled on top of her, raging with the sweet need of her, plunging fast and deep, arching and driving with pure, primitive passion. The savage was unleashed.

He drove into her, thrusting and rocking out of control, fighting for release as her shattering cries of climax echoed around him. And then he followed her, lost in a brilliant splendor, a beast who had tasted the food of the gods, flying free on the wings of glory.

TEN

"Your bedroom is . . . nice," Faline said, nestling her head in the strong, comforting curve of Brand's arm. They were tangled together in the sheets, body fitted against body as the morning sun streamed in through the windows, casting a dreamy glow throughout the room. It was a perfect reflection of how Faline felt inside. Warm and misty and a little unreal, as though her entire world was in soft focus.

"Nice," Brand agreed in a rusty, sleep-clouded voice, wrapping a possessive arm about her waist and pulling her closer.

"No, I mean, I didn't really notice it last night. I was"—her face colored slightly—"distracted."

He trailed a finger down the length of her arm. "Wildcat, you were *distracting.*"

She smiled to herself and snuggled into the smooth cotton sheets, her eyes still focused on the simple furnishings. There was a spartan realism about the room that was peaceful and reassuring—the large dresser hewn from rough wood, the natural-colored walls, the simple ceiling fan. *The man in the bed next to her.* She could imagine waking up like this forever.

She sighed, closing her eyes, trying to imagine how heavenly it would be. But she couldn't just pick up her life and transplant it to Florida. *Or could she?* It might take some serious career adjustments, some heartfelt rethinking about her personal and professional obligations, but it was an option.

She wondered what Brand would say if she suggested it. If she told him she was more content than she'd ever dreamed possible, that she wasn't sure she wanted to return to New York. Not now. Not when the photos were finished, not ever.

But something made her hold back. She wasn't ready to discuss the future, just yet. She was too busy reveling in the sweet reality of the present, too busy basking in the memory of last night's passion. Perfect, heart-stopping passion.

She hugged her arms to her chest and gave a quick shiver of delight.

"Cold?" he asked, drawing a blanket around her. "I don't usually sleep with a comforter, but"—he looked down at her—"I could get used to it."

Faline's heart tightened hopefully at the words, her throat aching from the effort not to laugh with joy. Their eyes locked for one quick, defenseless moment. "There are lots of ways to warm a body up," she responded quietly. "We may have to experiment a little."

He smiled slowly. "A little *more*, you mean."

She nodded, flushing.

He trailed light kisses down the side of her neck, then concentrated on her mouth. His long hair fell across her breast, tickling slightly, and his skillful fingers tenderly stroked her cheek. But just when things were starting to get good, he raised his lips from hers.

"It's a crying shame we can't spend the entire day in bed, Faline. But you have only a few days left to get the rest of the photos done."

Only a few days left. Did he have to remind her?

She tried to smile, but a halfhearted nod was all she could manage. Her heart felt suddenly heavy, as though every pulse was pumping her warm blood away, replacing it with cool, congealing lead. But maybe it was better that he had reminded her. Better for both of them.

She'd strayed a little too far into that dream world where anything was possible. She'd hoped that she might be able to stay forever. She'd hoped that he might ask her. But maybe she'd been expecting too much too soon. It was time to put everything into perspective, to keep her focus sharp. Time to get back to reality.

"Should be a lot easier now that Fang's decided to cooperate," she added lightly, sitting up.

He laughed, releasing his hold on her. "Cooperate? He's putty in your hands. Your biggest problem at this point will be to keep him from slobbering all over the camera."

She smiled and rose from the bed, draping the sheet around her as she reached for her robe.

She could feel his eyes following her across the room.

"And if you don't get yourself dressed quick," he added, his voice a soft, sensual whisper, "*I* may be the one to start slobbering. Guess we're both putty in your hands."

She flashed him a grin. "Not from what I remember."

He rubbed his chin thoughtfully. "Poor choice of words. Let's just say you make it hard to maintain control."

She threw the sheet at him and raced back to her own room. Sinking down onto the bed, the one that hadn't been slept in for two nights, she hugged her arms across her chest. Brand wasn't the only one who was losing self-control.

For a few memorable minutes, she'd been willing to do anything to stay at Wildacre Ranch. She'd been ready to rearrange her whole life just to be with him. For a few memorable minutes, she'd completely lost her mind.

Or maybe it wasn't her mind that she was in danger of losing.

"Great!" Faline exclaimed, focusing her camera on a wonderful, watery shot of Fang in the swimming pool. She snapped the shutter and advanced the film forward. Another perfect photo—the *Eco* editors would love it. Another perfect day at the ranch. *She* was loving it. Loving every precious minute of her time with Wildman Weston.

Over the past few days he'd definitely lived up to that crazy nickname. Brand was wild all right, *wild in bed.* Or to be more accurate, he was wild *out* of bed.

She flushed warmly, remembering every offbeat, primitive place they'd made love. The backyard pool, for instance. She'd never known that swimming could be so sensual. And on the wide, low branches of the old oak tree. They'd been sitting there for nearly an hour, photographing the lions as they roamed free about the yard, when Brand took the camera from her hand and showed her the sweetest way to spend an afternoon.

She'd had the sensation of floating on a cloud, shaded by the dense green leaves, her back supported by the sturdy trunk. He'd taught her a whole new way to experience lovemaking. And given an entirely new meaning to the word *balance.*

She lowered her camera and smiled at him, the vision still fresh in her mind. She felt a quiver of surprise as he left Fang soaking in the pool and came toward her, reaching out a hand to caress her cheek. She sensed the pulse that throbbed in his fingertips, beating strong and seductive against her sun-warmed skin. Desire surged within her, so quick and insistent it was almost scary.

This kind of passion was all new to her. The fierce longing, the white-hot awareness of her own need for him. The feeling was so intense, so overpowering that one touch could stimulate her to the point of arousal.

"Woman, you know what happens when you look at me that way."

His eyes locked with hers, and she realized that he knew. Exactly what she'd been thinking about. Exactly what she wanted at that very moment. She'd never known a man who could sense her excitement so completely. "Refresh my memory."

He took her by the hand and led her around the house and into the wooded jungle. It was wild and overgrown, richly studded with low palms and tropical flowers, the ground densely carpeted with soft ferns. It was so beautiful, so exquisitely sensual, that she closed her eyes for a moment, trying to commit every last twig and grain of sand to memory.

It was a picture that she knew would stay with her forever, to treasure and savor with all the others. But it was a memory that would grow sharp and bittersweet. Sooner or later, when it was time to leave, she would have to file all the pictures away.

Brand studied her expression. "Ever made love on a forest floor?"

She picked a bright fuchsia hibiscus blossom from a low bush and tucked it behind her ear, then wet her lips, smiling up at him. "I'm willing to give it a try."

He took her in his arms and settled her down on a soft bed of ferns. "Just let me know when you like it."

She sighed as he started to strip her blouse away. "I like it."

Faline was ready by the time her clothes were off. She was more than ready. She was *urgent.* She wanted to be taken immediately, to be crushed against the ground by his body, drowned in the feel of him. There was a fever in her belly, a fire lit by the depth of his passion.

Brand knew he wouldn't take it slow this time. He *couldn't.* There was nothing nice and civilized about the way he spread her legs, nothing sweet or seductive about the way he entered her. He penetrated her with a rough, unbridled intensity, thrusting hard, sinking himself fully inside her. This time there was no holding back.

Faline moaned, raking her fingernails down the straining muscles in his back, and thought she would die of ecstasy. She was pinned under him, her body arching, shuddering and helpless with sensation. He was plunging so deep within her, driving so hard and fast, she was burning up inside. Her soul was in flames.

Brand's hunger was just as hot, just as insatiable. He was a starving man, who couldn't get enough of a woman. *His woman.* He wanted to leave his mark on her with every exquisite thrust, to stake his territory, bury his seed inside her. He drove harder, pulling her close as the climax came over them, rocking and clutching her so tightly, he wasn't sure if he could ever let go.

And the moment he was peaking he knew he didn't *want* to let her go. He'd broken his own unwritten rule where wild creatures were concerned. He'd let his heart get involved. He'd made her his own.

When the final throes of passion had subsided, she nestled against him, and he bent to kiss the top of her forehead. He stroked the brown silk of her hair, swearing softly to himself. He was a damn fool. A damn fool who was going to pay like hell for his mistake. And this time it was a big one. He'd forgotten to remind himself that Faline was just passing through.

And sooner or later, no matter how much it hurt, he would have to set her free again.

He wouldn't allow himself to hold on this time, the way he had with Katrina. He could barely remember what his old fiancée looked like at the moment, but he could still feel the pain of being left again. It had happened once too often.

Katrina, his mother, they were only bitter memories now. But Faline was there and real and warm. And God help him, already a part of him. A part that would have to be cut out. A wound that would have to be cauterized.

This time, he swore in silent agony, *he* would do the letting go. It was the only way for a man to protect himself. The only way for a hermit like him to keep from getting burned.

"Faleeene!" The voice came from the vicinity of the house, cutting into Faline's satiated consciousness, breaking the peaceful, daydream quality of the afternoon.

"Is that Mrs. Twitchford?" she asked drowsily, guiltily hoping she wouldn't hear the voice again.

"Faleeene!"

Brand groaned and made himself sit up. "It must be important. Normally, Twitchford won't dare set foot outside"—he smiled softly—"luckily. But she has been known to call from an open window. Could be some darkroom problem?"

She shook her head and sat up reluctantly. "I'm sure I left everything in order." She trailed a hand across his chest, twining her fingers in the soft mat of blond hair, dropping them to his belly, to the top of the triangle where the hair grew coarse and several shades darker. "Maybe we could stay here just a little while longer?"

He clamped a hand down hard over hers. "Faline, you are insatiable. Not that I have any objections. But the sound of Mrs. Twitchford screaming your name could be a little distracting. We'd better go check it out."

She sighed, retrieving her clothes, and did her best to shake the sand out of them. Dressing hurriedly, she ran her fingers through her hair, picking bits of fern from the stray strands. "My friends in New York would never believe this."

He'd just finished pulling his jeans on, and he stopped to look at her, his expression unreadable. "Then you'll have something interesting to talk about when you get back."

She met his eyes, a little hurt. "It's not something I would ever discuss."

He shrugged and started toward the house. "Guess it'll just be a memory, then."

She swallowed hard, her throat constricting with emotion. "Guess so."

Mrs. Twitchford's urgent news turned out to be worse than a darkroom disaster. Much worse. Vail was waiting on the line from New York, with information so "*imperative,*" he'd badgered the housekeeper into believing it couldn't wait.

Faline picked up the phone. "Hey. It's me."

"*Hey?* Faline, honey, you're scaring me again. For a minute there you sounded like someone named Eliza Belle, or Jemmilou, or even Ellie May."

She scowled at the receiver, then answered sweetly, "Nope. It's just little old me."

"Don't tease me now, Faline. The thought of you in a calico dress and bare feet"—he choked loudly—"well, it just isn't funny."

She wondered what he would think about her in a rumpled blouse, with leaves in her hair and sand in her shorts. But she pushed the picture out of her mind. She really didn't care what he thought about it.

"Anyway," Vail continued, oblivious to her silence, "I have some super news, sweetie. Just super. Guess what it is."

She took a deep breath and forced herself to exhale slowly. "I could be a finalist in the million-dollar-sweepstakes giveaway?"

He sighed. "You're not going to guess, are you?"

"No, I'm not. And you *are* going to tell me what it is before I hang up."

"Spoilsport. It's an assignment, snook-ums. A plum assignment. Now, *puhleese* tell me you've finished with the beasts down there. All of them."

Her eyes flicked across the kitchen to Brand. He was leaning against the counter, his arms crossed in front of him, looking so devastatingly handsome, it made her stomach muscles knot. He was so beautiful, it hurt.

"I just finished today," she admitted reluctantly.

As soon as she'd said it, Brand left the room. Faline watched him in anguish as he walked away, wanting to reach out, to call him back, but Vail was still talking, dragging her attention back to the phone.

"Well hallelujah, honey, that is the best news I've heard all week. Because you've got to get back here immediately."

She closed her eyes, almost afraid to ask. "Immediately?"

"Like tomorrow, sweetie, if not sooner. You're back on top again. *We're* back on top. You won't believe the deal I made on this one. It's a corporate client, *Fortune* fifty, no less, but very in tune with the art scene. And guess what you'll be shooting? Office chairs. They want to make a statement about the chair as a work of art. Tweed, Naugahyde, secretarial, executive, they want serious art shots of all of them. Now, what I was thinking . . ."

Faline had a little trouble following the conversation after that, but through it all, one fact remained perfectly clear. It was time for her to leave Wildacre Ranch. Time to leave Brand and Fang and all those memories behind. To try to build her life all over again in New York. She'd taken the last roll of film, several more rolls, in fact, than she'd originally planned to, and she couldn't delay the inevitable any longer.

She wrote down the time and number of the flight reservations that Vail had made for the following morning and hung up the receiver with a sick, queasy feeling of finality. It was over. All over. Unless . . .

She shivered, and made her way into the darkroom to finish up the last of her photo proofs.

She needed to take them to Brand, to get his final approval and a photo release for their use, but she knew that was just a formality. What she really needed was a chance to talk to him. To tell him what was happening. And to hope like hell that he would ask her to stay.

A short while later she found him in the dining room, brooding over a glass of wine, his booted legs resting on top of the long table, his chair tipped back. He was perfect. *Perfect enough to make a woman fall in love.*

"So you're finished," he said quietly.

She nodded. "I thought you'd want to take a look at the proofs." She spread them out on the table.

The memories were all there, in beautiful, glossy reality. The lion pride at dusk with the male surrounded by his harem, Fang at play with his favorite beach ball, the panther mother and cub disappearing into the Everglades. Faline smiled at the cub's curious expression, remembering the moment. Remembering every moment she'd spent over the past two weeks.

She looked at Brand who had tipped his chair forward and was casually fanning through the photos. His eyes stopped on the picture of the cub, but his expression didn't change, and he finished the inspection with only one comment. "You're a gifted photographer."

Faline bit her lower lip, grateful for the compliment, but a little shocked by his impersonal tone. Hadn't he felt anything from the pictures? Didn't he remember the moments as vividly as she did?

The time they'd spent together had been so intimate, so intense, that Faline knew she was changed forever. She'd been metamorphosed into some new being, a woman less afraid to take risks, more aware of her own sensuality. He'd helped her to become that woman. Hadn't the experience meant anything to him?

"So they're what you expected?" she asked, feeling a little desperate.

He nodded, but he still wasn't looking at her. "They're dynamite. Better than I expected. It was worth all the effort, wasn't it?"

His voice was so cool and removed that Faline felt a tremor of fear run through her. *Worth the effort?* Is that how he'd felt about it? About her? As though it had been a chore?

She sank into a nearby chair, a wave of nausea flooding over her. "I'll need you to sign a photo release," she said after another minute of awful silence. "Just a formality giving your permission to use the pictures."

"Sure," he agreed, taking the paper and pen that she'd produced, scribbling his bold signature across it.

Brand Weston. A man Faline thought she'd understood. Not the cold stranger who was sitting next to her. Where had her passionate Wildman gone?

"So the job's finished, then. You'll be leaving."

It was a statement, not a question. She'd been

hoping that he would ask her to stay. Instead, he was practically telling her to leave.

She swallowed hard. Her throat had gone suddenly dry and tight. "My agent made plane reservations for tomorrow at ten." *Tomorrow.* Didn't he understand what she was saying?

When he didn't respond immediately, she added, "I can call a cab . . ." She was still clutching at some last shred of hope that he would object. Still grasping at air. She tried to laugh. "Although I wonder if they'd actually come get me. This place isn't exactly a tourist attraction. Well, you know what they call it. 'The Lion's Den' . . ."

His eyes were so detached and indifferent when he finally looked at her that Faline was stunned.

"I'll drive you," he said flatly. "Do you need any help getting packed?"

What she needed was a moment to collect her thoughts, to try to make some sense of what was happening. She remembered what she knew about his mother's desertion, the bitterness in his tone when he'd told her how his fiancée had taken off too. Even Mrs. Twitchford, the only loyal woman he'd ever known, seemed allergic to everything on the property.

But surely he must realize that she was different. Or maybe she hadn't made it perfectly clear how she felt. Maybe he didn't realize she wanted to stay.

He'd taught her to take risks, to trust in her

own instincts. She knew she couldn't have been that wrong about him. She had to keep talking, to help him understand. "I could change my reservations, stay awhile longer."

"What for?"

A surge of helplessness washed over her. She didn't stand a chance in the face of such cool bluntness. At least *his* feelings were crystal clear. He didn't see any reason to prolong her visit. He was good and ready for her to get the hell out.

She walked to the window, her lip trembling. Tears formed in her eyes, salty and bitter, but she couldn't hold them back completely. It was too hard to keep the feelings in check, even though it hurt to show him how much she was suffering. She wasn't allowed to get all sloppy and emotional. She was Faline, the professional. Faline, the seasoned photographer. Ms. Eastbrook, the strong, street-smart lady.

But she couldn't forget that for two memorable mind-blowing weeks, she'd been Brand Weston's woman. His Wildcat.

She brought her voice under control, but couldn't stop the tears entirely. Her eyes were still bright with them when she turned back to face him. "I guess there isn't any reason to stay, after all."

His voice lowered to a soft whisper. "Hell, Faline, don't cry. Don't make it any harder. You're tough, remember?"

She stared at him, her heart sinking. Oh, she

was tough, all right. So tough she wasn't about to admit the depth of her own pain. She was much better at blocking it out, pretending it wasn't there.

Even after Scott's betrayal she'd acted stronger than she'd felt. She'd been the one to reassure Vail that the business would recover. She'd been the one to promise her *friends* that the scandal would soon blow over. But it all seemed a little silly now, compared to this. Compared to the staggering intensity of her feelings for Brand.

"Go on, Wildcat. Run upstairs and pack."

The harshness in his tone ripped at her heart, but the name he'd used sparked a flicker of hope. *Wildcat.*

There had to be a reason he'd used that word. *Habit*, she thought reluctantly. Nothing else. So, why couldn't she just let it go, and disappear gracefully upstairs like a well-mannered houseguest who'd overstayed her welcome?

Because she didn't want to run along and do the sensible thing the way she always had. She didn't want to give up until she'd done all she could.

She put a hand on his arm. "If you change your mind—"

"For God's sake, Faline, *don't*!" A muscle worked in his jaw as he stared at her, his eyes blazing.

He was a wildman again, but not hers. Maybe he never had been. The man who'd rescued her from a tiger and shared unspeakable passion with her was gone. Vanished, as suddenly as the panthers. *Just passing through.*

She reached for the photo release and pictures, and left the room without another word.

ELEVEN

The sight of Faline boarding the plane hit Brand with the impact of a lightning bolt. Watching her leave was the toughest thing he'd ever done. The cool handshake she gave him, her purposeful stride as she walked away—they were hard to take without stopping her.

But he damn well wouldn't ask her to stay. Not this time. Trying to keep her on the ranch, to keep her with him, would only postpone the inevitable, only prolong the pain.

He'd understood the laws of nature from the beginning. He'd known she would bolt sooner or later. Experience at least had taught him that much.

Even if he did convince her to stay, she wouldn't realize what she'd be getting herself into. The confined, backwoods seclusion of his ranch couldn't possibly compare to the freedom of a big city. She'd be giving up a lot to remain with him, living a life of relative captivity. He couldn't keep her under those conditions. No matter how much he wanted her to stay.

The time he'd had her had been incredible. The kind of passion they'd shared, the soul-shattering intimacy had nearly blown him away. But he'd known all along it was too damn good to last forever. It was time to admit he'd never really had her at all. She could never be completely his. He had to do what was best for both of them and let her go.

He watched her hand her ticket to the gate attendant, gripping tightly the handle of her precious camera bag, clutching it as though she would never let go. Her face was pale, but free of tears. She hadn't shed a single one all morning, but Brand knew she was hurting underneath. He despised himself for causing her that pain.

She hesitated a moment before boarding, and looked at him one last time. Her eyes were bright with unspilled tears.

A sharp agony raked across Brand's heart. The impulse to follow her was so strong, he had to dig his hands in the pockets of his jeans to keep himself from reaching out. But a second later Faline had entered the plane and disappeared from his sight.

He walked over to the plate glass window, studying the big jet that would take her back to New York, to her own environment. He put his fist on the glass, wishing he could shatter it into a million pieces. But stopping her now would only bring more grief. He had nothing to offer her.

They came from completely different worlds. Faline was destined for better things than life on a nowhere ranch. She'd probably become a renowned photographer, and marry some cultured suit who could appreciate her art, some urban *gentle*man with nice, safe manners. She wasn't meant to be the wife of a barbarian.

He shoved his hands back in his jeans pockets and watched the jet taxi down the runway. Faline was going to be all right. But as for Brand Weston, the Wildman—he turned from the window and felt a numbness wash over him—the Wildman was alone again. And that was exactly the way he liked it. No permanent ties, no women around to worry about. Just the freedom of his ranch and the challenge of his animals.

Another abandoned cat would come along soon, another creature that needed rescuing. And he would be there to save it. The same as always. He threw a final glance over his shoulder and watched the jet rising into the sky.

She'd just been passing through. He couldn't afford to let himself forget that again. For two crazy weeks he *had* forgotten it, and it was costing him plenty now. For those two weeks he'd completely lost his head. He'd mistakenly imagined that someone had finally come along to rescue *him.*

A stupid idea. Downright ludicrous. Savages

didn't need saving. Barbarians were better off alone.

The drive back to Wildacre was a long one, maybe the longest of his life. The house echoed with a familiar silence when he walked inside. The same barren silence he'd grown used to before she'd arrived.

But the quiet was far more noticeable now, pervading everything about the place. And there was nothing in sight to alleviate it. There was only the future to contend with and the memories of her, and the aching monotony of the years that stretched before him.

He mounted the stairs and entered his bedroom. The scent of her was still there, and he wanted to take it in one last time. To take it in and put the past behind him. To find a way to face that self-sufficient future and admit that the savage inside would never be the same. To sever all ties with the Wildman within.

He glanced briefly in the dresser mirror, pulled a camping knife from his top drawer and positioned it at the base of his long, cord-tied ponytail. And cut his hair short with a single, sharp-edged stroke.

"*Corporate Jungle* is definitely my favorite."

"What?" Faline was jerked out of her daydream by Vail.

"*Corporate Jungle*," he repeated in exasperation. "The name of the chair with the animal-print cover. You photographed it, Fal, don't you remember?"

She shrugged lightly and sank back in her seat as he continued flipping through her latest portfolio. "They're *chairs*, Vail. I just took their pictures. I didn't bother to memorize their names."

"Grouch."

"Sorry."

He sniffed at the apology and continued scanning through her recent work. She'd been busy since her return to New York two weeks before, too busy to dwell on what she'd left behind. But every once in a while, some silly, unwelcome reminder came along, jarring her memory, triggering her pain. The word *jungle*, for instance.

She sighed and let the heartache take hold of her. She had to let it in occasionally, experience the hurt a little at a time. It was the only way to keep it from building up, from gathering strength until it was too much to handle. Sometimes the pain snuck up on her by surprise, and the force of it was so staggering, she wasn't sure if she could go on functioning normally.

What was he doing now? she wondered. Feeding the lions? Playing tug-of-war with Fang? Did he think about her at all? The questions were eating her up inside.

Her biggest doubt was still whether she'd made the right decision about leaving. What if she had *insisted* on staying, in spite of Brand's protests?

Looking back with a clearer head, she was even more sure that he had been reacting from his own pain and fears. Perhaps if she'd dug in her heels, he would have responded differently. Maybe he would have admitted that he wasn't completely independent, after all.

She swallowed hard to keep her throat from tightening up. She was clutching at straws again. Whatever the reason—misplaced nobility, or just plain disinterest, he'd asked her to go. He'd *told* her to go. It was sheer self-torture to keep replaying their last scene together. No matter how she looked at it, the ending was always the same.

She shook her head and tried to concentrate on what Vail was saying. She couldn't possibly have remained in Florida, even if she'd been gutsy enough to do it. Her career was definitely on the rise. New York wanted her, even if Brand Weston did not. She was one hot photographer. Faline, the queen of the office chairs.

"Fal, you're drifting again."

"Was I? Just thinking about that jungle number."

Vail lifted one skeptical eyebrow at her, but he didn't pursue it. "Speaking of the jungle, sweetie, I had a brilliant idea about what to do with those Tarzan pictures."

She narrowed her eyes at him. "I thought you said they were useless."

He looked up, spreading his lean arms wide.

"Fal, since when do you listen to everything I say?"

She smiled a little. "So what's this brilliant idea?"

He thrummed his long, narrow fingers slowly against her desk, building the suspense, milking the moment for all it was worth. "Are you ready? I think we should throw a little shindig here. Invite all of the old friends and clients and show them what you're capable of. We'll put the Tarzan photos on display, let everyone have a look at your latest, greatest work. Remind them you're still a fine photographer, even better off without Scott."

Faline shook her head doubtfully. "Not those photos, Vail. Couldn't we show them something else?"

He pursed his lips, and Faline recognized the familiar stubborn streak. It was going to be tough, if not altogether impossible to convince him.

"You're kidding, right? They're powerful, provocative. They're your best stuff, and you know it."

She nodded. "I know it."

"You must share the experience," he added dramatically.

Share it? She was trying like crazy to forget it. She followed his gaze to the back of the portfolio where she'd tucked the "provocative" photos away. Brand was in every one of them, looking more like some gorgeous retouched fantasy than a real life man she had actually met. Met and made love with.

The feelings flooded back to her. Her body responded involuntarily to the visual cues. The golden eyes, the strong, powerful muscles and long, gleaming hair. And even though it was only a memory, even though *he* was only a memory, she could still feel herself being pulled in. She could still feel those arms wrapped protectively around her, the hair tickling sensuously against her skin, the eyes burning into hers.

The pictures were more than provocative to her. They were painful.

"It's a nice idea, Vail, but I just don't think I'm up for a party."

He folded his arms across his chest, staring at her in exasperation. "A nice idea? Sweetcakes, it's a career necessity. You've got to get yourself back out there. Your work needs to be seen."

When she didn't respond, he asked gently, "Do you want to talk about it, Fal?"

Faline blinked hard, and suddenly realized that her eyes were filled with tears. Overflowing with tears. She couldn't stop them. She didn't even care to try.

"There isn't much left to talk about, Vail. He ended it."

Vail shook his head in disbelief. "Faline, you didn't really want to stay there with him, did you? Sure the body's to die for. But he's not exactly your type."

Always accurate, her agent. Of course Brand Weston wasn't her "type." He was a man who wouldn't fit into any mold. He was a rough, untamed individualist and unlike anyone she had ever met. Maybe that was why those two short weeks had been so painfully perfect.

"It doesn't make any difference now, Vail. It's over." *Over*, she repeated silently. She was through with lions and tigers and wildmen.

Maybe the "shindig" wasn't such a bad idea after all. It would give her a chance to close that chapter in her life. One last look at those photos—a well-organized, very public look—and she could say good-bye for good.

Vail squeezed her hand in encouragement. "The party would be good therapy, Faline. Get you back in the swing of things," he urged. "You never know what might come of it."

She nodded thoughtfully. The *Eco* article wouldn't come out for several months yet. In the meantime, the animals might benefit from the other photos being seen. A man and a tiger. Two ferocious beasts together. If the public felt just a twinge of the emotions she'd experienced from the sight, if she increased awareness only a little, it would be worth it.

She lifted a hand to her face, carefully wiping the tears away. "All right. Just when should we set this brilliant idea of yours in motion?"

Vail nodded in approval, gave her a quick, reassuring smile, then put his hands to his temples and started planning. "Next Friday night. Now, don't worry, you're doing the right thing. Trust me, it's going to be great."

"Fal, you look *fabulous.*"

Faline smiled at Vail's effusive compliment as she entered her studio, hung her wrap on the coat hook, and started setting out the hors d'oeuvres in final preparation for the party. She did feel extraordinarily feminine, if not exactly fabulous. The dress she wore was bright fuchsia, the color of the hibiscus blossom, and its slim, whispering folds wrapped her body in a vibrant sheath of silk. She still had some of her tan from the Florida sunshine, and her brown hair had taken on some striking blond highlights.

Vail frowned, biting his lower lip as he puzzled over her, critiquing her appearance from head to foot. "I don't know what it is exactly, snook-ums, but you've changed."

She gave a quick, rueful smile, acknowledging the observation. Vail was right. She *had* changed. Those two weeks at Wildacre had opened up her world, made her more aware of herself, of her attractiveness as a passionate, sensual woman. But the most profound differences were internal ones.

She'd formed an abiding, very personal understanding of love—intense, earth-shattering love. The kind that could help a woman grow from innocence to maturity. Or tear her heart in two.

She'd learned to take a chance again, learned

that risk had its own rewards, win or lose. Brand had taught her to trust in herself, to follow her own instincts, to make her own path in life. He'd taught her it was okay to trip and stumble along that path as long as you were willing to pick yourself up again and keep walking forward. But the most important thing he'd taught her was that the choice was entirely hers.

And she knew the right one to make tonight. To take what she'd learned and use it to move on with her life. No, she didn't feel exactly *fabulous*, but she did feel strong enough to face the future. Her new inner awareness had helped her do that.

The crowd was already milling around the room in their basic black couture, sipping cheap champagne, devouring canapés, and gazing with keen interest at her work. Twenty of her best photos had been dramatically enlarged, framed, and matted in the minimalist style.

Words like "interesting," "primitive," and Vail's favorite, "provocative," were faintly audible over the rising din. Faline scanned the room, a little amazed and very amused. The party was off to a perfect start. They liked her work. But suddenly it didn't seem important.

The same crowd who'd deserted her so many weeks ago was now ready to hail her as the latest and greatest. But the only opinion she cared about was that of a man who wasn't here. Brand. God, how she missed him.

She couldn't help it. The visual reminders of him were everywhere. As well as verbal ones.

"Who is he?" she heard a woman whisper behind her. And, "Oh *my.*"

Faline's smile was bittersweet. They were talking about the Wildman, with exactly the same words she'd used once. The photos were definitely having an effect on people. Now if she could only get over the effect they were having on her . . .

"He's *divine,*" another voice said. "All that gorgeous hair."

Faline closed her eyes, some of her newfound strength starting to ebb. She'd expected her clients and colleagues to admire the photos, as well as the man in them, but a whole evening of such candid reminders could be agonizing.

And enlightening. She took a sip of champagne and forced herself to face the pictures again. It was the only way to get over it. To get over *him.*

She studied them one by one, trying to take it all in, to make some sense out of what had happened between them. There was Brand with the lions, Brand protecting her from Fang, Brand next to the panthers before he'd let them go.

He'd made it look so simple, turning loose the mother and cub, watching them walk away forever. Faline hadn't realized it then, but she knew it had to have been hard on him, harder than he wanted to admit. He'd gotten so good at saying good-bye, that he'd learned to make it look easy.

The same way he had when *she* had walked

away for the last time. The same way he had when *she* had said good-bye.

Was it possible that he'd been hurting as well?

He'd clammed up that last night at the ranch. Shut her out so completely, she couldn't get close enough to tell what he was feeling. He'd practically pushed her away.

She scanned the photos again, remembering the times he'd stepped in to protect her, sheltering her body with his. Was that what he'd been trying to do that night? To protect her one last time? From the ranch? From him?

She'd been a fool not to see it. A fool not to realize that even a man as tough and brave as Brand Weston could still be afraid of something. Afraid that *he* might be the reason women always left. Afraid to find out by asking her to stay.

He'd chased her away intentionally, trying to save them both.

If you love something, set it free . . . It was a saying she'd read a long time ago, but it had stuck with her through the years. Somehow, she had to prove that she wanted to come back to him.

She set her champange glass on a nearby tray, motioning to Vail as she grabbed her purse and wrap. He walked over to her, a look of alarm on his aristocratic face.

"What is it, sweetness? Don't you feel well?"

She kissed him lightly on the cheek. "I feel terrific. For the first time in weeks. Forgive me for leaving so early, but I need to go."

"Go?" He shot her a stunned look. "Go where?"

She gave him a long hug and a sympathetic smile. "I'm going to my apartment to pack and to make some plane reservations."

"Fal, you're not going back to the swamps again? Back to him?"

She opened the studio door, throwing him a farewell smile over her shoulder. "I'll call, I promise. But I have to go back where I belong."

"You say he won't eat anything?"

Brand shook his head, and followed Marshall through the woods and over to Fang's cage. It wasn't like the tiger to turn away food, and that was what had him so worried. After two days of the odd behavior, he'd finally called in the vet.

"Not even chicken necks," Brand added, casting a concerned glance at the sleeping cat. Fang sure didn't look sick, but he had been acting extra skittish lately. Ever since—

"Any temperature?" Marshall asked.

"Normal," Brand responded, watching the even rise and fall of the tiger's respiration. At the sound of his voice the big cat stretched and stood up, waiting expectantly.

"Let him out then, and we'll have a closer look."

Brand released Fang from the cage, then stood back as Marshall proceeded with the examination.

Doc Ryder was a top-notch vet, and Brand had to step in only once when Fang began to look a little irritated. As a rule, tigers were not the most patient of patients.

"Down, Fang."

Marshall grinned his thanks. "I sure as hell am glad it was you who took that temp instead of me."

Brand barely cracked a smile.

"Walk him around once," Marshall suggested, his eyes studying Brand as intently as they were watching the tiger.

Brand complied, signaling Fang with his voice and hands, skillfully directing the great cat into a wide, slow circle.

"You can put him back in his cage," the doc said after a minute or so. "I've seen enough."

Brand's eyebrows went up, but he complied. He turned to Marshall, his voice heavy with concern. "Find something?"

Marshall nodded. "There is something wrong. But it isn't with the tiger."

Brand threw him a challenging look. "What the devil are you talking about?"

Marshall scratched his chin, thoughtful. "Let me put it this way, *Wildman.* Have *you* been eating anything lately?"

"For chrissake, Ryder, you're a vet, not a psychiatrist. Lay off, okay?"

"You wanted a professional opinion, right? Well, I'd say this animal's in perfect health. Perfect physical health. The only thing ailing him is you."

"What is that supposed to mean?"

Marshall folded his arms across his chest. "Take a good look at yourself, Weston. You're going off the deep end—and taking poor Fang here with you."

The tiger looked up at the sound of his name, blinking at Marshall in complete concurrence.

Brand groaned, but the doc continued, unmerciful. "You haven't shaved in two weeks, you probably haven't eaten either, and you look like hell. You're determined to live up to your reputation now, aren't you?"

Brand gave him a long warning look. "And exactly how does my physical appearance relate to Fang's well-being, *Doctor*?"

"Elementary, my dear Weston. He won't eat because he senses how upset you are. Now go ahead and tell me you're just fine."

Brand hesitated. He sure as hell didn't feel fine. But he knew there wasn't a thing Ryder could do to help him. Not unless there was some new miracle remedy for a hermit with a broken heart. "I'm fine."

"Liar."

"Quack."

Marshall dropped his hands to his hips. "Be nice, or I won't cure Fang."

"You just told me there was nothing wrong with him."

"Not exactly. I said there was something wrong with you."

Brand's jaw tightened perceptibly, his mouth twisting into a cynical smile. "*That* you definitely can't cure."

Marshall shot a quick glance toward his mobile vet van, smiling enigmatically. "Don't be so sure."

Brand followed the direction of his gaze and frowned. There was a woman stepping out of the van. Another woman on his ranch. The last thing he needed right now.

He narrowed his eyes suspiciously at the doc. "If this is your idea of treatment, Ryder—" He stopped. The air was knocked out of him suddenly when the woman turned and he was finally able to see her face.

Faline. She was here. And she was walking toward him.

He turned to Ryder, swearing softly. "You fool. You don't understand. Get her *out* of here."

Marshall shook his head. "Sorry, pal. This wasn't my idea. It was hers. All I did was give her a lift from the airport. It was the least I could do. Now, the least you can do is take your medicine like a good boy and don't blow it."

But Brand didn't get the opportunity to respond. By the time he got his breath back, Marshall was already driving away in the van. And Faline was directly in front of him. Within arm's length. It took every last ounce of strength he had not to pull her close.

But instead of touching her, the way he wanted

to, he folded his arms across his chest and asked her bluntly, "What the devil are you doing here?"

Faline took a deep breath. Once before she'd had to face her fears and go to him, to prove she truly trusted him. This time it was twice as hard.

Brand looked angry, his face rough and unshaven, his eyes bright and bitter. It was scary to see the change in him. The ponytail was gone, but somehow he seemed more savage than ever, like some magnificent rogue male she'd stumbled upon in the forest. She didn't know how he would react to her words. The only thing she did know was that she had to trust in her instincts. To let go and take one final, fatal risk.

"I love you," she told him simply.

Their eyes locked and held. Faline felt her heart bump hard against her chest as the smoky glow of his gaze burned into hers.

"You *shouldn't*," he told her, his voice ragged. "I'm bad news. Past history proves it. Take a warning, woman, you'd better get out while the getting's still good."

Faline didn't budge. She knew better than to let him chase her off this time. Her gut feeling about him had to be right. "Too late," she answered firmly. "I'm not leaving."

"Maybe I didn't make myself clear last time. I *wanted* you to leave."

"It's no good," she told him. "The only way I'm going is if you tell me you don't love me. If you really want to get rid of me, it's simple enough."

He raked the hair back from his eyes, hesitating, his face full of anguish. Faline could see the struggle going on inside. She held her breath, waiting in hope and joy as he fought against his own words.

"You want to hear it? All right. I do love you. I love you so damn much, I had to let you go. Now, *leave.*"

Faline's heart was so full, she couldn't speak. He loved her. Nothing else mattered. She was strong enough to stand anything now. She put a hand to his face and trailed her fingers softly across the hard, handsome surface of his cheek. "Never," she whispered.

He let out a low groan and caught her hand in his, pressing it roughly against his face. "Don't do this to me, Wildcat. I can only fight you for so long."

"Then listen to your own advice," she told him, her eyes wide and wet with unshed tears. "Don't try to fight it. Just go with it."

"I have to be sure, Faline. What made you decide to come back?"

"Faith," she answered. "You gotta have it. You're the one who taught me what it's all about. Faith and trust. It's the best thing between us."

He drew back, catching both of her hands in his. "You're sure this is what you want? To stay at the ranch? For good? For better or worse?"

For better or worse? More beautiful words were never spoken. Faline wanted to melt into his arms, but first she had to understand why he'd wanted her to leave. She needed to hear him say it. "Brand," she whispered, tightening her grip on his hands. "About my last night at the ranch—"

"Faline, I didn't want you to go. I thought I had to make you leave."

He shook his head slowly, trying to explain. "I'd gotten so used to good-byes, I couldn't accept the fact that it might end up differently with you." A muscle tightened in his jaw. "I guess I started to believe that the ranch wasn't the problem at all. That maybe the problem was me. I got very good at chasing people away. Long before they had a chance to leave."

"I know," she whispered.

He let go of her hands and wrapped his arms around her waist, pulling her tight until their bodies melded together. "Faline, you still haven't answered my question. Will you stay with me for better or worse and be my wife? Will you marry me?"

Her breath caught. She felt the strength in his body, read the promise in his eyes, and wondered how she'd lived without him for the last few weeks. She was stunned to realize she hadn't lived. She'd been sleepwalking. Through a nightmare. And now she'd finally woken up to the sweetest dream of her life.

"Yes," she told him, and meant it the way she'd never meant anything before. "I will."

He cupped her face with his hands. "God, how I've missed you. I couldn't get you out of my mind. It's true that women don't seem to stick around at Wildacre. But maybe they just haven't been the *right* women. The right woman."

"And am I?" she asked, a little breathless. "The right woman?"

He flashed her a slow grin. "Lady, you've sure been the gutsiest. You're the only one who's ever gotten close to Fang. I think he was trying to tell me something all along. I just wasn't wise enough to listen."

"Fang?" she asked, smiling. "Did he miss me too?"

He walked her over to the big cat's cage, unlatched the door, and let Fang do the talking himself. The tiger strolled out, padded patiently toward Faline, and gave her hand several long, slobbery licks.

Faline bent down to give him a hug. "Thanks for the welcome home, old boy."

Brand pulled her up into his arms again. "I should've known better than to argue with a tiger," he told her. "He tried to communicate with me. He went off his food for a while—staged a hunger strike to try and bring you back."

Faline shot the big cat a look of concern. "Is he okay now?"

Brand smiled slowly, lazily. His voice was

rough and sensual when he spoke. "Wildcat, everything's okay now."

Her pulse skyrocketed. She felt the warmth spreading from her cheeks all the way down to her toes. The memories started flooding back to her, brief snapshots of time flashing quickly through her brain. The Wildman's body in the moonlight, dripping wet. A drowsy wildman lying beside her in bed.

"Watch out, woman," he warned softly. "You know what happens when you look at me that way."

She tilted her head back, closing her eyes in invitation. But Brand didn't need one. He was already there. He let out a low moan and fitted his mouth to hers.

Faline's lips parted under his sweet, insistent persuasion, and the kiss intensified, strong, savage, mind-shattering.

But just when it was starting to get good, Brand drew back. "Sure you want to marry me?"

She nodded. "Positive. Now, where were we?"

But he held off. "What about your work?"

She smiled. "A camera is a wonderful thing. Completely portable."

"You're too talented to give it up, you know. I'd be willing to share you with New York for short periods. In case you needed to go back on business."

She was close to crying again, deeply touched by his concern for her career.

She put her hand up to his hair, to the short blond locks swept back from his face. Still loose and sunswept. Still shockingly handsome. "What happened here?"

Brand shrugged. "Call it a symbolic gesture. A new beginning."

Faline nodded, then her eyes widened as a sudden thought struck her. "I can just imagine what Vail is going to do about all this. He'll probably launch a publicity campaign—*Tarzan Holds Photographer Captive in Secluded Love Nest.*"

"Tarzan?"

She grinned mischievously. "That's what he calls you."

"How flattering. Maybe we should have him down for a visit. I'll introduce him to Fang."

She bit her lower lip. "You wouldn't!"

"I might. Unless you can domesticate me first."

She shook her head. "Guess Vail will have to take his chances. I'd rather keep you wild."

He stroked the side of her cheek, looking hard into her eyes. "Faline, you *make* me wild."

Her heart caught in her throat as she imagined every slow, exquisite moment they would share tonight. Only now the moments stretched before her into endless, blissful oblivion. Tonight was only the beginning.

She ran her hands through his hair again, sighing as it flowed free and loose through her fingers. She met his golden gaze, unblinking, and started to work on his T-shirt, splaying her hands under it, across the smooth, bronzed surface of his chest. Brand groaned, burying his face in her hair, growling with unrestrained passion.

The Wildman was free again, sexy, untamed. A savage unleashed. But Faline knew they were mated for life. And she wasn't afraid any longer.

THE EDITORS' CORNER

Along with May flowers come four fabulous LOVESWEPTs that will dazzle you with humor, excitement, and, above all, love. Touching, tender, packed with emotion and wonderfully happy endings, our four upcoming romances are real treasures.

Starting the lineup is the innovative Ruth Owen with **AND BABIES MAKE FOUR**, LOVESWEPT #786. Naked to the waist, his jeans molded to his thighs like a second skin, Sam Donovan looks like trouble—untamed and shameless! Dr. Noel Revere hadn't expected her guide to the island's sacred places to be so uncivilized, but this rebel sets her blood on fire and stirs her insides like a runaway hurricane. Can they survive a journey into the jungle shared by two matchmaking computers with mating on their minds? Once again,

Ruth Owen delivers an exotic adventure that is both wildly sexy and wickedly funny!

In her enchanting debut novel, **KISS AND TELL**, LOVESWEPT #787, Suzanne Brockmann adds a dash of mystery to a favorite romantic fantasy. When Dr. Marshall Devlin spots Leila Hunt alone on the dance floor, he yearns to charm the violet-eyed Cinderella into his arms, but how can he court the lady when they fight over everything, and always have? Then the clock strikes twelve and Leila is possessed by the passion of a familiar stranger. He captures her lips—and her soul—in a moment of magic, but can she learn to love the man behind the mask?

From award-winning author Terry Lawrence comes **FUGITIVE FATHER**, LOVESWEPT #788. A single light burned in the window of the isolated lakeside cottage, but Ben Renfield wondered which was the greater risk—hiding in the woods to evade his pursuers or seeking refuge with a beautiful stranger! Touched by his need, tempted by her own, Bridget Bernard trades precious solitude for perilous intimacy . . . and feels her own walls begin to crack. Can rescuing a lonely warrior transform her own destiny? Terry Lawrence blends simmering suspense and stunning sensuality in a tale that explores the tender mysteries of the human heart.

Finally, there's **STILL MR. & MRS.**, LOVESWEPT #789, by talented newcomer Patricia Olney. Two years before, they'd embraced in a heated moment, courted in one sultry afternoon, and wed in a reckless promise to cherish forever. Now Gabriel and Rebecca Stewart are days from the heart-breaking end of a dream! When a business crisis demands a last-minute lover's charade, Gabe offers Reb anything she wants—but will their seductive game of "let's pretend" ignite flames of dangerous desire? In this delicious story of second chances, Patricia Olney makes us believe in the enduring miracle of love.

Happy reading!

With warmest wishes,

Beth de Guzman

Shauna Summers

Beth de Guzman	Shauna Summers
Senior Editor	Editor

P.S. Watch for these Bantam women's fiction titles coming in April: From the *New York Times* bestselling author Betina Krahn comes another blockbuster romance filled with her patented brand of love and laughter in **THE UNLIKELY ANGEL.** Also welcome nationally bestselling author Iris Johansen in her hardcover debut of **THE UGLY DUCKLING,** a tale of contemporary romantic suspense! **DANGEROUS TO HOLD** by Elizabeth Thornton is filled with her trademark passion and suspense, and **THE REBEL AND THE REDCOAT** by Karyn

Monk promises a scorching tale of passion set against the dramatic backdrop of the American Revolution! Be sure to see next month's LOVESWEPTs for a preview of these exceptional novels. And immediately following this page, preview the Bantam women's fiction titles on sale now!

Don't miss these extraordinary books
by your favorite Bantam authors!

On sale in March

MYSTIQUE

by Amanda Quick

DIABLO

by Patricia Potter

THE BAD LUCK WEDDING DRESS

by Geralyn Dawson

A tantalizing tale of a legendary knight and a headstrong lady whose daring quest for a mysterious crystal will draw them into a whirlwind of treachery—and desire.

From *New York Times* bestseller

Amanda Quick

comes

MYSTIQUE

When the fearsome knight called Hugh the Relentless swept into Lingwood Manor like a storm, everyone cowered—except Lady Alice. Sharp-tongued and unrepentant, the flame-haired beauty believed Sir Hugh was not someone to dread but the fulfillment of her dreams. She knew he had come for the dazzling green crystal, knew he would be displeased to find that it was no longer in her possession. Yet Alice had a proposition for the dark and forbidding knight: In return for a dowry that would free Alice and her brother from their uncle's grasp, she would lend her powers of detection to his warrior's skills and together they would recover his treasured stone. But even as Hugh accepted her terms, he added a condition of his own: Lady Alice must agree to a temporary betrothal—one that would soon draw her deep into Hugh's great stone fortress, and into a battle that could threaten their lives . . . and their only chance at love.

From the winner of the Romantic Times *Storyteller of the Year Award comes*

DIABLO

by **Patricia Potter**

Raised in a notorious outlaw hideout, Nicky Thompson learned to shoot fast, ride hard, and hold her own against killers and thieves. Yet nothing in her experience prepared her for the new brand of danger that just rode in. Ruggedly handsome, with an easy strength and a hint of deviltry in his smile, Diablo made Nicky's heart race not with fright but with a sizzling arousal. When she challenged him to taste her womanly charms, she didn't know he was a condemned convict who'd come to Sanctuary with one secret purpose—to destroy it in exchange for pardons for himself and a friend. Would a renegade hungry for freedom jeopardize his dangerous mission for a last chance at love?

With a sigh of pure contentment, Kane relaxed in the big tin bathtub in an alcove off the barber's shop. One hand rubbed his newly shaved cheek. The barber had been good, the water hot. The shave had been sheer luxury, costing five times what it would have in any other town, but that didn't bother him. In truth, it amused him. He was spending Marshal Ben Masters's money.

He lit a long, thin cigar that he'd purchased, also at a rather high price. He supposed he was as close to heaven as he was apt to get. Sinking deeper into the water, he tried not to think beyond this immediate pleasure. But he couldn't forget his friend Davy. The leash, as Masters so coldly called it, pulled tight around his neck.

Reluctantly, he rose from the tub and pulled on the new clothes he'd purchased at the general store. Blue denim trousers, a dark blue shirt. A clean bandanna around his neck. The old one had been beyond redemption. He ran a comb through his freshly washed hair, trying to tame it, and regarded himself briefly in the mirror. The scar stood out. It was one of the few he'd earned honorably, but it was like a brand, forever identifying him as Diablo.

Hell, what difference did it make? He wasn't here to court. He was here to betray. He couldn't forget that. Not for a single moment.

With a snort of self-disgust, he left the room for the stable. He would explore the boundaries of Sanctuary, do a reconnaissance. He had experience at that. Lots of experience.

Nicky rode for an hour before she heard gunshots.

She headed toward the sound, knowing full well that a stray bullet could do as much damage as a directed one. Her brother Robin was crouching, a gunbelt wrapped around his lean waist, his hand on the grip of a six-shooter. In a quick movement, he pulled it from the holster and aimed at a target affixed to a tree. Then he saw Nicky.

The pride on his face faltered, and then he set his jaw rebelliously and fired. He missed.

Nicky turned her attention to the man next to him. Arrogance radiated from him as he leered at her. Her skin crawling, she rode over to them and addressed Cobb Yancy. "If my uncle knew about this, you would be out of Sanctuary faster than a bullet from that gun."

"That so, honey?" Yancy drawled. "Then he'd have to do something about your baby brother, wouldn't he?" He took the gun from Robin and stood there, letting it dangle from his fingers.

Nicky held out her hand. "Give me the gun."

"Why don't you take it from me?" Yancy's voice was low, inviting.

"You leave now, and I'll forget about this," she said.

"What if I don't want you to forget about it?" he asked, moving toward her horse. "The boy can take your horse back. You can ride with me." His hand was suddenly on the horse's halter.

"Robin can walk back," she said, trying to back Molly. Yancy's grasp, though, was too strong.

Yancy turned to Robin. "You do that, boy. Start walking."

Robin looked from Yancy to Nicky and back again, apprehension beginning to show in his face. "I'd rather ride back with you, Mr. Yancy."

The gun was suddenly pointed at Robin. "Do as I say. Your sister and I will be along later."

Nicky was stiff with anger and not a little fear. "My uncle will kill you," Nicky pointed out.

"He may try," Yancy said. "I've been wondering if he's as fast as everyone says."

Nicky knew then that Cobb Yancy had just been looking for an excuse to try her uncle. Had he scented weakness? Was he after Sanctuary?

She felt for the small derringer she'd tucked inside a pocket in her trousers. "Go on, Robin," she said. "I'll catch up to you."

Robin didn't move.

"Go," she ordered in a voice that had gone hard.

Softness didn't survive here, not in these mountains, not among these men.

Instead of obeying her, Robin lunged for the gun in Yancy's hand. It went off, and Robin went down. Nicky aimed her derringer directly at Yancy's heart and fired.

He looked stunned as the gun slipped from his fingers and he went down on his knees, then toppled over. Nicky dismounted and ran over to Robin. Blood was seeping from a wound in his shoulder.

She heard hoofbeats and grabbed the gun Yancy had been holding. It could be his brother coming.

But it wasn't. It was Diablo, looking very different than he had earlier. He reined in his horse at the sight of the gun aimed in his direction. His gaze moved from her to Robin to the body on the ground.

"Trouble?"

"Nothing I can't handle," Nicky said, keeping the gun pointed at him.

The side of his mouth turned up by the scar inched higher. "I see you can," he said, then studied Robin. "What about him?"

"My brother," she explained stiffly. "That polecat shot him."

"I think he needs some help."

"Not from you, mister," she said.

His brows knitted together, and he shifted in the saddle. Then ignoring the threat in her hand, he slid down from his horse and walked over to Robin, pulling the boy's shirt back to look at the wound.

Robin grimaced, then fixed his concentration on Diablo's scar. "You're that new one," he said. "Diablo."

Diablo nodded. "Some call me that. How in the hell did everyone around know I was coming?"

"There's not many secrets here," Robin said, but his voice was strained. He was obviously trying to be brave for the gunslinger. Nicky sighed. Hadn't he learned anything today?

Diablo studied the wound a moment, then took off his bandanna and gave it to Robin. "It's clean. Hold it to the wound to stop the bleeding."

He then went over to Cobb Yancy, checked for signs of life and found none. He treated death very casually, Nicky noticed. "He's dead, all right," Diablo said.

Before she could protest, he returned to Robin. He helped Robin shed his shirt, which he tore in two and made into a sling. When he was through, he offered a steadying arm to Robin.

"Don't," Nicky said sharply. "I'll help him."

"He's losing blood," Diablo said. "He could lose consciousness. You prepared to take his whole weight?"

Nicky studied her brother's face. It was pale, growing paler by the moment. "We'll send someone back for Yancy. He has a brother. It would be best not to meet him."

Diablo didn't ask any questions, she'd give him that. She looked down at her hands and noticed they were shaking. She'd never killed a man before.

Diablo's eyes seemed to stab through her, reading her thoughts. Then he was guiding Robin to Yancy's horse, practically lifting her brother onto the gelding. There was an easy strength about him, a confidence, that surprised Nicky. He'd looked so much the renegade loner that morning, yet here he'd taken charge automatically, as if he were used to leadership. Resentment mixed with gratitude.

She tucked the gun into the waist of her trousers

and mounted her mare. She kept seeing Yancy's surprised face as he went down. Her hands were shaking even more now. She'd killed a man. A man who had a very dangerous brother.

She had known this would happen one day. But nothing could have prepared her for the despair she felt at taking someone's life. She felt sick inside.

Diablo, who was riding ahead with Robin, looked back. He reined in his own horse until she was abreast of him, and she felt his watchful gaze settle on her. "Tell Yancy's brother I did it."

Nothing he could have said would have surprised her more.

"Why?"

"I can take care of myself."

He couldn't have insulted her more. "And what do you think *I* just did?"

"I think you just killed your first man, and you don't need another on your conscience. You certainly don't need it on your stomach. You look like you're going to upchuck."

She glared at him. "I'm fine."

"Good. Your brother isn't."

All of Nicky's attention went to Robin. He was swaying in his saddle. She moved her horse around to his side. "Just a few more minutes, Robin. Hold on."

"I'm sorry, Sis. I shouldn't have gone with . . . Cobb Yancy, but—"

"Hush," she said. "If you hadn't, Yancy would have found something else. He was after more than me."

But Robin wasn't listening. He was holding on to the saddle horn for dear life, and his face was a white mask now.

"Maybe I should ride ahead," she said. "Get some help."

"You got a doctor in this place?" Diablo asked.

"Not right now. But Andy—"

"Andy?"

"The blacksmith. He knows some medicine, and I can sew up a wound."

"Go on ahead and get him ready," Diablo ordered. "I'll get your brother there." He stopped his horse, slipped off, and then mounted behind Robin, holding him upright in the saddle.

Could she really trust Diablo that much? Dare she leave him alone with Robin?

"I'll take care of him," Diablo said, more gently this time.

Nicky finally nodded and spurred her mare into a gallop.

Wearing it was just asking for trouble

THE BAD LUCK WEDDING DRESS

The most memorable Texas romance yet
from the uniquely talented

Geralyn Dawson

"One of the best new authors to come along in years—fresh, charming, and romantic!"
—*New York Times* bestselling author Jill Barnett

They were calling it the Bad Luck Wedding Dress, and Jenny Fortune knew that spelled trouble for her Fort Worth dressmaking shop. Just because the Bailey girls had met with one mishap or another after wearing Jenny's loveliest creation, her clientele had begun to stay away in droves. Yet Jenny was still betting she could turn her luck around—by wearing the gown herself at her very own wedding. There's just one hitch: first she has to find a groom. . . .

While people all over the world have strange ideas about luck, Fort Worth, being a gambling town, seemed to have stranger ideas than most. Folks here made bets on everything, from the weather to the length of the sermon at the Baptist church on Sunday. Jenny theorized that this practice contributed to a dedicated belief in the vagaries of luck, making it easy for many to lay the blame for the Baileys' difficulties on the dress.

Monique shrugged. "Well, I think you're wrong. Give it a try, dear. It's a perfect solution. And you needn't be overly concerned with your lack of a beau. Despite your father's influence, you are still my daughter. The slightest of efforts will offer you plenty of men from whom to choose. Now, I think you should start with this."

She pulled the pins from Jenny's chignon, fluffed out her wavy blond tresses, then pressed a kiss to her cheek. "I'm so glad I was able to help, dear. Now I'd best get back to the station. Keep me informed about the developments, and if you choose to follow my advice, be sure to telegraph me with the date of the wedding. I'll do my best to see that your father drags his nose from his studies long enough to attend."

"Wait, Monique," Jenny began. But the dressing-room curtains flapped in her mother's wake, and the front door's welcome bell tinkled before she could get out the words "I can't do these back buttons myself."

Wonderful. Simply wonderful. She closed her eyes and sighed. It'd be just her luck if not a single woman entered the shop this afternoon. "The Bad Luck Wedding Dress strikes again," she grumbled.

Of course she didn't believe it. Jenny didn't believe in luck, not to the extent many others did, anyway. People could be lucky, but not things. A dress could not be unlucky any more than a rabbit's foot could be lucky. "What's the saying?" she murmured aloud, eyeing her reflection in the mirror. "The rabbit's foot wasn't too lucky for the rabbit?"

Jenny set to work twisting and contorting her body, and eventually she managed all but two of the buttons. Grimacing, she gave the taffeta a jerk and felt the dress fall free even as she heard the buttons plunk against the floor.

While she gave little credit to luck, she did believe rather strongly in fate. As she stepped out of the wedding gown and donned her own dress, she considered the role fate had played in leading her to this moment. It was fate that she'd chosen to make Fort Worth her home. Fate that the Baileys had chosen her to make the dress. Fate that the brides had suffered accidents.

The shop's bell sounded. "*Now* someone comes," she whispered grumpily. "Not while I'm stuck in a five-hundred-dollar dress and needing assistance." She stooped to pick the buttons up off the floor and immediately felt contrite. She'd best be grateful for any customer, and besides, she welcomed the distraction from her troublesome thoughts.

Pasting a smile on her face, Jenny exited the dressing room and spied Mr. Trace McBride entering her shop.

He was dressed in work clothes—black frock jacket and black trousers, white shirt beneath a gold satin vest. He carried a black felt hat casually in his hand and raked a hand nervously through thick, dark hair.

Immediately, she ducked back behind the curtain.

Oh, my. Her heart began to pound. Why would the one man in Fort Worth, Texas, who stirred her imagination walk into her world at this particular moment?

She swallowed hard as she thought of her mother's advice. It was a crazy thought. Ridiculous.

But maybe, considering the stakes, it wouldn't hurt to explore the idea. Jenny had the sudden image of herself clothed in the Bad Luck Wedding Dress, standing beside Trace McBride, his three darling daughters looking on as she repeated vows to a preacher.

Her mouth went dry. Hadn't she sworn to fight for Fortune's Design? Wasn't she willing to do whatever it took to save her shop? If that meant marriage, well . . .

Wasn't it better to give up the dream of true love than the security of her independence?

Jenny stared at her reflection in the mirror. What would it hurt to explore her mother's idea? She wouldn't be committing to anything.

Jenny recalled the lessons she'd learned at Monique's knees. Flirtation. Seduction. That's how it was done. She took a deep breath. Was she sure about this? Could she go through with it? She *was* Monique Day's daughter. Surely that should count for something. She could do this.

Maybe.

Trace McBride. What did she really know about him? He was a businessman, saloon keeper, landlord, father. His smile made her warm inside and the musky, masculine scent of him haunted her mind. Once when he'd taken her arm in escort, she couldn't help but notice the steel of his muscles beneath the cover of his coat. His fingers would be rough against the softness of her skin. His kiss would be—

Jenny startled. Oh, bother. Had she lost her sense entirely?

Perhaps she had. She was seriously considering her mother's idea.

What was she thinking? He'd never noticed her before; what made her think he'd notice her now? What made her think he'd even consider such a fate as marriage?

Fate. There was that word again.

Was Trace McBride her fate? Could he save her from the rumor of the Bad Luck Wedding Dress? Could he help her save Fortune's Design?

She wouldn't know unless she did a little exploring. Was she brave enough, woman enough, to try?

She was Jenny Fortune. What more was there to say?

Taking a deep breath, Jenny pinched her cheeks, fluffed her honey-colored hair, and walked out into the shop.

On sale in April:

THE UGLY DUCKLING
by Iris Johansen

THE UNLIKELY ANGEL
by Betina Krahn

DANGEROUS TO HOLD
by Elizabeth Thornton

THE REBEL AND THE REDCOAT
by Karyn Monk

OFFICIAL RULES  **NO PURCHASE NECESSARY**

To enter the sweepstakes outlined below, you must respond by the date specified and follow all entry instructions published elsewhere in this offer.

DREAM COME TRUE SWEEPSTAKES

Sweepstakes begins 9/1/94, ends 1/15/96. To qualify for the Early Bird Prize, entry must be received by the date specified elsewhere in this offer. Winners will be selected in random drawings on 2/29/96 by an independent judging organization whose decisions are final. Early Bird winner will be selected in a separate drawing from among all qualifying entries.

Odds of winning determined by total number of entries received. Distribution not to exceed 300 million.

Estimated maximum retail value of prizes: Grand (1) $25,000 (cash alternative $20,000); First (1) $2,000; Second (1) $750; Third (50) $75; Fourth (1,000) $50; Early Bird (1) $5,000. Total prize value: $86,500.

Automobile and travel trailer must be picked up at a local dealer; all other merchandise prizes will be shipped to winners. Awarding of any prize to a minor will require written permission of parent/guardian. If a trip prize is won by a minor, s/he must be accompanied by parent/legal guardian. Trip prizes subject to availability and must be completed within 12 months of date awarded. Blackout dates may apply. Early Bird trip is on a space available basis and does not include port charges, gratuities, optional shore excursions and onboard personal purchases. Prizes are not transferable or redeemable for cash except as specified. No substitution for prizes except as necessary due to unavailability. Travel trailer and/or automobile license and registration fees are winners' responsibility as are any other incidental expenses not specified herein.

Early Bird Prize may not be offered in some presentations of this sweepstakes. Grand through third prize winners will have the option of selecting any prize offered at level won. All prizes will be awarded. Drawing will be held at 204 Center Square Road, Bridgeport, NJ 08014. Winners need not be present. For winners list (available in June, 1996), send a self-addressed, stamped envelope by 1/15/96 to: Dream Come True Winners, P.O. Box 572, Gibbstown, NJ 08027.

THE FOLLOWING APPLIES TO THE SWEEPSTAKES ABOVE:

No purchase necessary. No photocopied or mechanically reproduced entries will be accepted. Not responsible for lost, late, misdirected, damaged, incomplete, illegible, or postage-die mail. Entries become the property of sponsors and will not be returned.

Winner(s) will be notified by mail. Winner(s) may be required to sign and return an affidavit of eligibility/release within 14 days of date on notification or an alternate may be selected. Except where prohibited by law, entry constitutes permission to use of winners' names, hometowns, and likenesses for publicity without additional compensation. Void where prohibited or restricted. All federal, state, provincial, and local laws and regulations apply.

All prize values are in U.S. currency. Presentation of prizes may vary; values at a given prize level will be approximately the same. All taxes are winners' responsibility.

Canadian residents, in order to win, must first correctly answer a time-limited skill testing question administered by mail. Any litigation regarding the conduct and awarding of a prize in this publicity contest by a resident of the province of Quebec may be submitted to the Regie des loteries et courses du Quebec.

Sweepstakes is open to legal residents of the U.S., Canada, and Europe (in those areas where made available) who have received this offer.

Sweepstakes in sponsored by Ventura Associates, 1211 Avenue of the Americas, New York, NY 10036 and presented by independent businesses. Employees of these, their advertising agencies and promotional companies involved in this promotion, and their immediate families, agents, successors, and assignees shall be ineligible to participate in the promotion and shall not be eligible for any prizes covered herein. SWP 3/95